KV 66

SIPTAH'S LEGACY

A GEORGE DRAKE NOVEL

K G M A W

Printed in the United States of America

ISBN: 979-8-504080-31-4

*To my dear wife, Sherry, who has always been
an inspiration and given me the confidence
to do battle in commerce and encouraged my
writing. I dedicate this book to her and also
our three daughters Natasha, Natalie,
and Tanya.
I would also like to thank my former employers
for giving me the freedom to pursue this
adventure, which has been built on my love of
Egyptian history and the Egyptian people,
who feel like family. This is a work of fiction.
Names, characters, businesses, events, and
incidents are the products
of the author's imagination.
Any resemblance to actual persons, living or
dead, or actual events is purely coincidental.*

PROLOGUE

1558 BC

With the arrival of the gods within the surrounding vicinity of Thebes, Upper Egypt was to become the powerhouse of the country. This was not the first time a pantheon from the vast array of immortals depicted on the nation's proud monuments had been sighted in the area, but it was the first time that one had decided to pay a visit and settle down in this tightly controlled environment.

Only a handful of the pharaoh's most trusted aides were ever privy to the secret of how they had traveled from the heavens in a ship crafted from an unknown metal. The vessel, which was circular in shape, also resembled the disk symbol of the great sun god Amun Re. The module's appearance fueled those few chosen religious intellects with a plethora of additional material, which only served to either strengthen their ideological positions or increase speculation over the origin of these mythological icons.

The strange yet beautiful craft had descended from the skies into a rugged valley just across the muddy river near the ancient city of Thebes. The Greek poet Homer had once described this enclave as the city of a hundred gates where four hundred heroes with horses and chariots had passed through in a military procession as he marveled at the precision-built architecture and wide avenues, much of which would be built in the post-disk period.

Thebes was built around the Temple of Karnak and considered the official sanctuary of the god Amun. Its high priest, a man by the name of Siptah, was fortunate enough to catch a glimpse of the disk as it soared over the city. Tracking its trajectory, he noted its exact point of impact in a deserted chasm just a few leagues away on the other side of the river.

At first he thought it was a shooting star, as the object trailed a characteristic long tail of flames. However, as it broke through the atmosphere and started plummeting toward the ground, he noticed how rounded it was—far too perfect to be anything but divine. Even though it fell at great speed, as it came nearer to impact, a strange force seemed to slow it down, almost as if it was trying to avoid the ultimate collision, and Siptah gazed in awe as the glowing ball cascaded into the valley wall.

With a handful of temple guards, he headed for his private stables where horses were always saddled and ready for use. With the guards trailing behind, he galloped off down the Avenue of Sphinxes to a point on the river bank holding the local ferry—a simple barge linked to both sides of the river by a rope on a pulley system. Once they had all clambered aboard, Siptah signaled the operator to pull them across. No sooner had the barge touched the opposite bank, the riders had already kicked their mounts into action and made off for the valley.

Unfortunately, it was too dark to make anything out, and to compound matters, the air was full of powdered dust and rock particles from the craft's heavy impact with the mountainside. Siptah decided to place a permanent guard post at the valley entrance and sent for Horemosis, who was currently residing at his palace in Memphis, the pharaoh and traditional seat of power of the kingdom. In his message Siptah beckoned the pharaoh to make all haste and witness firsthand the unearthing of this strange object that be believed had been dispatched by their divine deities.

Horemosis was young, handsome, and still unwedded. Uniting the northern and southern halves of his territory had preoccupied most of his thoughts for the past few years. The Nile, or Iteru as it was known during this period, which normally flooded the delta plains of Memphis, had failed to provide enough irrigation for their annual crops; consequently, his people were growing hungry. Thebes up to now had managed to stave off the shortfall. However, there was growing dissent among the nobility and increasing pressure on the young king to forsake his throne to a Theban and avoid a potential civil uprising.

Siptah, unlike the majority of Thebans, adored his king and desperately wanted him to relocate to Karnak and put an end to the unrest. This celestial offering from the heavens could be the catalyst for his cause, and Siptah anxiously awaited Horemosis's return.

Siptah arranged for one hundred of his temple guards to act as sentries and secure the entrance to the isolated valley, which had been carved out by rains long ago and had steep, rugged cliff faces covered with loose scree and sand. It was shaped like a human hand with fingers splayed and in the early morning sun glowed red, radiating off a mysterious energy. Dominating the canyon at the point of impact was a pyramid-shaped mountain peak known as Al-Qurn (the horn).

The next morning, Siptah clambered up the valley floor to the point where the disk had plummeted the night before. It was buried in a deep recess at the foot of the mountain having penetrated and exposed a natural cave system that had been carved into the rock face over many millennia. An avalanche of rocks and boulders had fallen making it hardly visible.

It would take laborers weeks to remove the debris, and with his mind, Siptah concluded that this sacred spot could also make the ideal burial site for his beloved Horemosis. The obscure location would eventually become known as the Valley of the Kings, and even though Horemosis would be its first eternal inhabitant, surprisingly, he would soon be forgotten.

Now convinced that this was the right path, Siptah ordered several hundred slaves to be brought to the valley and set them to work building the royal tomb, never to leave again.

Over the coming weeks, stonecutters worked on the sides of the opening while others erected a crude pulley system to remove the piled-up rocks. Siptah nervously paced each day while monitoring the progress.

Horemosis arrived by royal barge four weeks after work in the valley had commenced and requested that Siptah escort him to the tomb location to view the disk.

The stonecutters had done an excellent job chiseling out an entry point into a series of dark chasms where the disk now lay. As far as construction of the tomb was concerned, Siptah had decided he would need to tunnel further into the mountainside so his pharaoh's sarcophagus could be pulled deeper into a separate series of inner chambers, well protected from potential grave robbers in the years to come.

Horemosis asked Siptah to clear the area of all craftsmen and slaves, as he wanted to have some time alone to inspect the ethereal object. After everyone had left, Horemosis climbed up a crude wooden ladder and approached the strange, golden-colored body. What was this heavenly message, he wondered. Surprisingly the metal was warm to the touch even with the cool morning temperature. The saucer-shaped body had a smooth, bulbous top and despite the heavy impact with the rocky terrain showed no evidence of damage. It was not very big and only measured roughly three times his height from the ground up and about five times his height in diameter. From a small platform that had been erected adjacent to the craft, Horemosis leapt aboard and crawled up to its apex where he noticed what appeared to be a small crack in the metal. From his calf-leather belt, he withdrew a jewel-encrusted dagger and tried to slip the blade into the crack. Nothing happened. However, as he leaned on a section of the craft while trying to pull out the blade, he felt the metal under his palm give. The apex began to rise with a grating sound, uncovering what appeared to be an entrance.

Horemosis tightened the grip on his dagger, and fear enveloped him. "Siptah! The disk has spoken to us. Come quickly!"

Siptah, who had remained alone at the foot of the excavation, rushed over and ascended to the platform joining his king on the surface of the disc. Horemosis recounted how the apex had moved and asked Siptah if he would enter and reveal what the object contained. Siptah grabbed a small pottery lamp fitted with a linen wick hanging from one of the platform's wooden struts. The lamp burned oil mixed with salt to inhibit smoke. He handed the lamp to Horemosis and asked him if he could pass it down once he entered the disk through the narrow opening.

Having clambered inside he called for Horemosis to join him. It was not too dark as the walls glowed with brightly colored lights and a mysterious hum from below alerted them that there must be more to the object than what they were seeing. In the center of the room, they found another concealed opening with metal stairs leading down. Siptah slowly descended. The room was much smaller than the one above and contained what resembled two sarcophagi, each covered by metal lids. On the top of each lid was a lever, and not knowing what these signified, Siptah motioned to Horemosis to try and give them either a push or pull. Eagerly, the pharaoh applied a tight grip on the protruding mechanism and felt the lever give. As the lever clicked into position a hiss sounded, and ever so slowly the metal lid began to retract into the wall of the sarcophagus.

Siptah followed suit with the other lid, and both fell to their knees when they finally saw a body neatly tucked inside each box. Both were of a similar form to humans, and one was clearly female A glass panel, however, still sealed them in from the outside air.

Their skin color appeared pale and cold with no signs of life. The male was already in a state of decomposition, his pod inactive. However, in the case of the female, after the outer lid had slid open, lights flashed at the foot of her container. From inside, a glass protrusion with a sharp needle attached to it automatically maneuvered its way to her chest cavity and plunged deep into her sternum. They watched with fascination as a purple liquid was injected from the glass vial into her body. At the same time red lights flashed around the inner circumference of the lid, radiating a gentle heat. Moments later her fingers twitched as life was now being restored to the cadaver as the two Egyptians stared, bewildered by the process.

As the female's eyes opened shock registered on her face as she gazed back at the two strange-looking people on the other side of the glass. Her right-hand fingers reached out and touched a green switch retracting the glass panel separating her from the outside.

With life now restored and the mechanical processes complete, the room became silent once again, and not a word was ushered between Siptah and Horemosis as they continued to gaze down on this gift from the stars.

Breaking the silence, she called out in a language totally bizarre to them, but from the look of desperation on her face, they knew she was in distress.

Horemosis was captivated by the woman's stunning beauty. She had large, green eyes and high cheekbones. Unlike most Egyptians her hair was light brown and cut short. Her skull was also larger housing a significantly more advanced brain and an ability to absorb knowledge like a sponge. She also wore a strange, tight-fitting garment that accentuated her sensual contours and heightened his desire to keep her for himself within the confines of his palace.

It was some time before she had strength enough to emerge from her shell, and as she climbed out and looked over toward her partner, tears flooded her eyes, and she wept at her loss. Clearly, whatever had brought her back to the living had failed with the male. She pushed the lever back into its original position closing off the sarcophagus.

Unable to communicate in her strange tongue, the two Egyptians used hand signals and gestures to encourage the woman to follow them out of the roof exit. The woman, once out, depressed the hidden switch sealing the apex. Not a word was spoken as they made their way out of the valley, across the river, and back to Karnak where Horemosis occupied a small palace adjacent to the great Temple of Amun Re. To reach it, they traversed along the magnificent Avenue of Rams. Then, passing through the Great Hypostyle Hall, which housed the largest known columned structure in the world, they eventually reached the palace buildings located in the Sacred Lake area.

Guards acknowledged their king's presence and dropped to their knees as he approached. Once inside Siptah ordered a servant to bring food and drink, which they then offered to the woman continuing to communicate with childlike gestures.

In the months that passed Hatshepsut, as the woman was now aptly named, learned the language of the Egyptians and accepted that her life would end in this strange land. She was able to explain to Horemosis that both she and her partner were from another world far away on the other side of their sun. They had been traveling the stars in a much bigger "starship" in search of other life forms and had run into difficulties. Only the two of them had managed to avoid a fiery death and exit their stricken mother vessel in an escape pod, which ultimately crashed in the nearby mountain. She must have traveled many millions of miles within the pod in a carefully controlled deep state of sleep. Unfortunately the mechanism that kept her alive for all this time did not function correctly for her companion.

Hatshepsut would never meet her future great-granddaughter who ruled Egypt from 1479 BC to 1458 BC and became one of the greatest female warriors in history. She would also carry the same name as if anointed from the gods.

These were happy times, and Hatshepsut enjoyed walking through the town helping out wherever she could. Horemosis moved his court to Karnak, which also pleased Siptah who frequently accompanied Hatshepsut on her walkabouts. Her knowledge turned out to be immense. She was a highly skilled physician and knew how to open up the human body and perform surgical techniques. She instructed the armorers how to forge fine instruments and produce blades sharper than anything that had ever been seen before. Needless to say these skills were also adopted for military purposes, and as a result the Egyptians became more powerful and expanded their empire deep into the southern territory of Nubia.

Hatshepsut conducted lessons and introduced the concept of pathology to Egyptian doctors and taught them how to operate from the dissection of human corpses. A cool room adjacent to the temple was chosen as a makeshift medical school, and Hatshepsut became its first principal with no shortage of students anxious to take hold of these "magical powers." Preservation of the cadavers was not a problem as the chemicals needed for this purpose were the same as those used in ritual mummification; something the Egyptians had been practicing for thousands of years. However, Hatshepsut showed the priests how to refine these chemicals, making them far more effective in the preservation process, particularly for organs stored in alabaster jars. A scribe carefully documented all lessons so that in her absence, an assistant could take her place.

Hatshepsut's reputation grew. Royalty and wealthy nobles from far afield traveled to Karnak for medical consultations, which she provided. Some even consented to being operated on in order to ensure themselves a prolonged existence. Not once did she ask for any sort of compensation, and as a result she was treated like a goddess. Scribes took her work to the Temple of Kom Ombo and chiseled away images of her medical equipment and procedures to ensure they would be preserved for all time. Sacrifices were made to Isis, the great goddess of magic, and to Ra-Atum—Sun God, creator of the world, and whom many believed had delivered Hatshepsut to their community.

Almost twelve months after her arrival, all the gossip concerning Hatshepsut's mysterious appearance had disappeared, and she was now considered a key member of the Theban community. The fact that she was held in such high regard made Siptah increasingly jealous as his position had become almost secondary, and whenever Horemosis needed advice, it was Hatshepsut who provided him with the answer. Infuriated, he immersed himself with work on the tomb and was rarely seen in court.

Aided by the natural contours of the prehistoric cave system located within the mountainside, Siptah had now managed to build out a series of new tunnels and rooms in preparation of Horemosis's final resting place.

The first fifty yards consisted of a small narrow tunnel leading from a new concealed entrance excavated at the foot of the valley wall that fed into an immense system of caverns.

At the end of this first grotto, Siptah had fabricated a large ebony doorway that opened up into a further giant hallway, where he had instructed masons to fashion out a number of pillars to support the roof. In addition, he ordered the construction of a gigantic wall at the end of the hall that would be used to conceal Hatshepsut's metal craft within a section of cave remaining behind the wall.

To the right of the entrance hall, they carved out three other chambers which would be used to store many of the pharaohs most prized belongings. The last and final room, which was richly decorated with extracts from the *Book of the Dead*, was designated entirely for housing his sarcophagus at the time of his future burial.

Siptah had summoned Horemosis to the valley to inspect progress and also witness the sealing up of the disk. Hatshepsut accompanied the pharaoh and showed no sign of emotion as she watched. She had no wish to reenter the capsule or pay homage to her dead companion. Instead, she gazed intently as laborers heaved the disk into its final position at the end of the cave along with the platform that had first been used to gain access.

To camouflage the point where the disk was concealed, the bricked-up area was coated with several layers of plaster and merged in with the rest of the tunnel. Again sculptors and artists were brought in to cover the whole tunnel and annex areas with pictures of life under the rule of Horemosis.

Very soon, not one trace of the hidden room could be found. Only Siptah new its exact location, which he secretly recorded on a papyrus by making reference to the mural of Hatshepsut holding onto a sacred Ankh, which had been carved over the now walled-up entrance.

With the disk now well away from prying eyes, Siptah relaxed and concentrated on finishing off the remainder of the tomb. Two more years would be spent completing this task.

Shortly after the disk had been sealed away, Horemosis decided it was time to ask Hatshepsut if she would become his wife and queen. She eagerly accepted, and a date was agreed upon which would coincide with the Festival of Opet.

The Opet Festival came at a time of the year when the god Amun was dying, and the world was threatened with chaos. Actually, Amun had a double personality; the Amun who was worshipped in Karnak was the god of the sun and skies, whereas a few miles down the road at Luxor, the god Amun-Min was in essence a phallic god of fertility.

During the celebrations, a statue of the dying god would be taken from the Temple of Karnak and carried in a procession led by Siptah. Firstly, They would make their way down to the riverside onto a waiting barge, which would be towed by the royal boat to the Luxor Temple. Secret ceremonies would finally be conducted by the pharaoh, which would restore life back into the dying god and reaffirm the pharaoh's legitimacy as ruler.

Horemosis thought this would be a most fitting time for his marriage as not only would he be able to demonstrate his role as mediator between the gods and humanity, he would also be taking the hand of a goddess sent from the heavens.

Both Karnak and Luxor geared up for the celebrations, which were to last for two weeks. Thousands of gallons of beer and wine were brought in as well as the finest cattle for slaughter. Musicians and entertainers arrived from all parts of the Egyptian Empire.

On the wedding day Horemosis dressed in robes made from the finest linen and adorned the double crown of Upper and Lower Egypt. Hatshepsut was given equally splendid attire and wore on a gold crown molded in the shape of Horus and encrusted with Lapis.

As high priest, Siptah conducted the ceremonies of Opet (pushing aside his envy), with the marriage vows restoring life to their dying god. As the young couple emerged from the temple, they were besieged by people trying to get a glimpse of their king and queen. With cries of joy, the two living gods joined in the crowd and kicked off the festivities.

Horemosis escorted his new bride back to their royal quarters and ordered all the servants to leave them in seclusion. As it was customary for women to live in separate chambers, he had never until this day laid eyes on her naked body and wondered whether she had any physical differences from native Egyptians. Would the act of lovemaking be any different?

His excitement was evident as he felt himself stiffen. Hatshepsut moved closer and unclipped her robe. As it fell to the ground, her beautiful body was exposed revealing perfect contours. Sensing a little shyness in her new husband, she took his hand, led him to their bedroom, and took off his clothes. Pushing him back onto the bed, she took some perfumed oil and massaged his body, from his feet to his shoulders. Horemosis could hardly control his excitement as he took the oil and reciprocated the massage. Hatshepsut squealed with delight, and after more than an hour of foreplay, she rolled on top of him melting into a passionate embrace. They both screamed with delight as they climaxed in unison while gazing into each other's eyes and drifted into a loving sleep.

Horemosis was besotted with Hatshepsut and whenever possible would try to find time for further lovemaking. He couldn't believe how lucky he was to have such a beautiful and talented wife who was so sexually active. He learned all types of new ways to make love and enjoyed these lessons. Her passion was endless, and to evidence his true faithfulness, Horemosis set free all the palace concubines and said he would no longer look at another woman.

Hatshepsut accepted her new life and loved her husband. As queen of Egypt, she ceased practicing medicine and took on official duties. Here again she was able to put her superior knowledge to great use and introduce many ideas to improve the general quality of life of her people including techniques to improve the strength and durability of clothing and engineered better living quarters for all.

Siptah found his role in the couple's lives was becoming ever more superfluous and that his anger toward Horemosis was building. So much for gratitude!

As the days passed, Siptah's love for his king vanished and was replaced with a hate. He had decided that the only way for him to regain his position would be to kill the royal couple, but only after an heir had been produced. This way he would be able to act as guardian and rule the nation until the heir to the throne was ready to take over, by which time he would already be in total control.

Siptah did not have to wait too long; Hatshepsut became pregnant only a few months after the festival of Opet. The speed with which her fetus developed surprised almost everyone, and Siptah suspected that from wherever she came, the gestation period must be less than that of a human. By the sixth month, she began to show signs of severe stress and discomfort. It was during this time that she also began to bleed heavily. Horemosis maintained a vigil by her bedside only able to offer moral support.

By the middle of the seventh month, her contractions started. Hatshepsut was in great pain, and while midwives attended to the birth, Siptah offered her a sacred brew to kill the agony. With each contraction, Hatshepsut appeared to be getting weaker. Her fetus was certainly not premature in size, and when the head finally breached, it was extremely well formed.

Sadly, no one would realize that the medicine administered by Siptah was actually a potent potion designed to feign death and that as she pushed during her last contraction, her heart seized giving the impression that life finally had drained from her body.

Hatshepsut would never cast her beautiful green eyes on her newborn son, Ahmosis.

Horemosis grieved at her bedside as the midwives cut the cord and slapped the posterior of the newly arrived prince. As cries bellowed from the baby's tiny mouth Siptah made a discreet exit for the sanctuary of his temple and thought about masterminding stage two of his plan to usurp the pharaoh after instructing orderlies to remove the queen's body and send it to the temple for embalming.

A young woman who had recently given birth was chosen to suckle Ahmosis and moved into the pharaoh's palace. Her husband had been a general in the army and had died during the campaign to take back Nubia. Her full breasts held plenty of milk for both babies, and Ahmosis, while missing his natural mother, would have a friend to grow up with. The arrangement worked extremely well although Horemosis was clearly lost without Hatshepsut.

Siptah fueled his melancholy by constantly reminding him of what Hatshepsut had done in the past and how she had been a gift from the gods. He encouraged the pharaoh to drink wine to blur those memories, pushing him to the brink of a breakdown and also weakening his guard.

As high priest, Siptah said he would take care of Hatshepsut's funerary arrangements and would prepare a separate room for her in his tomb so that when Horemosis's time came, she would be close by.

Hatshepsut's body was taken to the Temple of Amun Re for mummification. The whole process would traditionally take seventy days, and now that the pharaoh was at his weakest, Siptah decided it was the perfect time to complete his act of treachery. As Hatshepsut's body lay still, Siptah invited Horemosis to the temple to oversee its transfer to the mummification chamber. Siptah had already secretly taken the pharaoh's jeweled dagger from the palace and kept it hidden within his robes. As the pharaoh knelt in front of Hatshepsut, Siptah crept up behind him and pulled the dagger out of its sheath. Standing behind the pharaoh, he whispered in his ear, "My king, it's time for you to join your wife. Please forgive me."

Horemosis was unsuspecting, and as the dagger penetrated his chest cavity, there was almost a look of relief on his face. He did not cry out or try to resist. As the blade reached his heart, he gasped as blood filled his lungs and found its way up through the trachea and began seeping from his mouth. Slumping forward his head came to rest on Hatshepsut's breasts.

To cover up any sign of foul play, Siptah carefully placed Horemosis's hands around the hilt of his dagger and rushed out of the temple distraught and screaming the news of the death of their king. Guards rushed to the scene, and as everyone knew of the pharaoh's grief, no one considered that this act could have been perpetrated by anyone other than the king.

Siptah had always had a secret love for Hatshepsut and would never have actually murdered her. Consequently, he felt that the only way to put an end to the Horemosis dynasty was to make the death appear real. Once Hatshepsut had been laid to rest in the temple, Siptah had removed her clothes and cleaned her up, as much blood had been lost through the act of labor. He then dressed her back up in the finest robes and placed in her hands a beautiful golden ankh as the symbol of everlasting life. To fool the mourning nation, he took the body of another woman of similar proportions to the queen and quickly commenced the mummification process.

Siptah elevated himself to the position of caretaker ruler and set to work preparing for the funeral. Embalmers then removed the internal organs and placed the liver, lungs, stomach, and intestines in sacred alabaster jars. The heart, which was believed to be the source of intellect, was sealed back inside both their bodies. Strangely, the brains were not considered important, and these were slowly drawn out through the nose by a suction process. As they were of no further use they were thrown away.

Following removal of the organs, the bodies were dried with salt, prior to a further washing, then coated with preserving resins. Rings were put on their fingers, gold crowns placed on their heads, and fine clothes over their bodies to make them more presentable for the journey into the afterlife. It was only after this that the wrapping process commenced in which hundreds of yards of linen would be used for each mummy.

With the mummification procedure complete, Siptah and his cortege of priests performed ceremonies in the major temples. The mummies were placed into a series of nesting coffins and made ready for their journey to the tomb. Each of the innermost coffins was made from solid gold and molded into the appearance of the king and queen. The outer coffins were made of wood; however, even these were highly decorated with gold leaf and semiprecious stones.

The coffins were transferred to a waiting boat and taken across the Nile. From there it would be a long trek by foot to the valley where their tomb had been long since prepared.

During the period of embalming, Siptah had made ready an additional stone sarcophagus cut from a block of granite and shaped into the form of Horemosis. The heavy stone container had to be carefully lowered through the tomb entrance and then, using a system of wooden rollers, moved down the passageway to the final burial chamber. In the chamber, a similar sarcophagus had already been positioned for the mummy of Hatshepsut. Once in place, a pulley system was erected and used to hold up both the giant lids so the coffins containing the mummies could be arranged inside and secured for their journey into the other world.

Following the procession came a whole flotilla of boats bearing priests and officials along with funerary furniture and personal belongings that would be sealed inside the tomb with the king and queen. Only a privileged few were allowed entry into the valley.

Siptah clutched the *Book of the Dead* that would be sealed inside the burial chamber alongside the two sarcophagi.

Siptah showed no remorse, and in his usual precise manner documented a full account of all the events to date along with the precise location of the tomb entrance. Although he had declared the valley a sacred place for kings to be buried after death, in so far as Hatshepsut and Horemosis were concerned, he decided to cover up the entrance with boulders and sand to prevent their final resting place from being desecrated by robbers. He knew all too well that the tombs of earlier pharaohs had all been pillaged and was determined that the secret of Hatshepsut should never be revealed.

His recordings were almost in the form of a confession, and rather than leaving them in plain sight Siptah decided to hide them in a secure location—the Temple of Sobek at Kom Ombo, where Hatshepsut had already made her impression by way of the recordings of her surgical techniques and instrument design. The last entry in the journal dealt with the disposal of Hatshepsut's body, which some time after Ahmosis's birth was taken from the temple in Karnak to the tomb of Horemosis where Siptah had arranged for a few carefully selected laborers to reopen the hidden room containing the golden disk.

Now, having once gained entry, he ventured back inside the disk for one final reunion with his precious celestial object, carefully carrying the queen's body.

Finding his way down the short ladder into the small cavity below, he opened the coffin-like structure from which she had initially appeared having remembered how they had activated it when they first set eyes on her.

Siptah's plan had gone like clockwork, and as he took his final look at Hatshepsut's beautiful face, he pulled back on the lever they had used to open the receptacle. Within seconds, he heard the same characteristic hiss of gas and whir of a mechanism inside commencing a cryogenic process that would place Hatshepsut into a deep state of preservation, which would last for as long as the fusion reactors held out onboard the escape pod now entombed within the Valley of the Kings. Indirectly he was embalming Hatshepsut with a mummification process that would outlast anything they could ever match with their primitive ritual methods.

With a shiver descending his spine that was partly fed by the guilt that raged within every pore of his body, he exited the craft, made his way back through the narrow opening, and instructed the laborers to seal up the entrance, replace the inscriptions, and remove all signs of the presence of this room. These laborers were expendable and would not live long enough to pass on their secret to potential tomb robbers.

Now that Siptah's power struggle was complete, he decided it was time to conceal all his personal recordings as planned and elected to make a short pilgrimage to the Temple of Sobek at Kom Ombo, which he had decided would be a fitting resting place for this documented journal.

Kom Ombo was a strategically important location south of Karnak used extensively during Horemosis's campaigns against the Nubians. The temple itself was located out of the town, and while it was more closely associated with Sobek, it also represented the falcon-headed god Horus. All features of the temple were in duplicate, the left side being for Horus and the right half for Sobek.

Adjacent to the entrance pylon was an additional building, known as the "birth house," and it was here that Hatshepsut had had her recordings carved into the walls. Running alongside this was an entrance to a narrow subterranean tunnel that extended downward to a large pool filled with crocodiles. The reptiles were free to venture in and out as they pleased from the neighboring "sacred" riverbank and were kept in honor of Sobek. Only the high priest was ever allowed to venture down this tunnel and only during a time of sacrifice.

It was perfect for Siptah, who by now had already removed one of the small limestone slabs and carefully dug out a hole in the side of the wall. Here he placed the scrolls having first secured them in a watertight jar wrapped in a crude leather hide. With the scrolls concealed, he replaced the slab and filled the cracks with a type of cement to prevent any chance of future detection. Just before leaving he crudely carved the cartouche of Horemosis onto one of the blocks as if it were an act of graffiti to mark the spot as a secret remembrance of his crime.

By accident a junior priest from the temple entered the tunnel just as Siptah was putting the final touches on his handiwork. The man, barely in his twenties, looked nervously at Siptah and asked what he was doing. Siptah approached slowly so as not to alarm him. Before the young man could utter a cry he thrust the dagger that had once belonged to the pharaoh deep into the chest of the priest. As he collapsed in a heap on the floor, a gurgling sound broke the silence, as bright-red, frothy blood spluttered from his gaping mouth.

To remove any evidence of this heinous act, Siptah tossed the body into the pool to the eagerly awaiting crocodiles. The moment the limp body hit the water, the ugly brutes ripped the carcass to pieces in a thrashing frenzy, turning the water into scarlet foam.

Turning away, Siptah checked the wall. Satisfied that the papyrus scroll was hidden from inquisitive eyes, he strolled back out into the blazing sunshine and headed off to the twin Temple of Horus to say a few prayers and remerge into the world as if nothing had happened.

Siptah ruled the empire until Ahmosis turned eighteen and reluctantly handed over the reins of power, as the young prince crossed into manhood.

Ahmosis, who would start off the dynasty of the New Kingdom, had an unusual disliking for Siptah, as if he knew of the treachery that had happened the year he was born. However, the country had remained stable throughout his rule, and his people were generally content.

Relegated to a position of obscurity, Siptah retreated to his temple and lived out the remainder of his life as a lonely recluse.

After Siptah's death two years later, Ahmosis decided to give him a burial fit for a ruler. He was buried in a small tomb located at the entrance to the sacred valley, which would ultimately become the burial place for all the kings and queens of the New Kingdom, the site unknowingly nominated by Siptah himself.

Among his possessions were a number of scrolls, one depicting the young pharaoh Horemosis taking a ship into the heavens. This drawing represented his journey into the afterlife. Underneath this drawing he had made some notations which consisted of four distinct messages. Firstly a symbol of the god Sobek followed by a drawing of a tunnel. After this was a measurement represented by fifty legs and finally a cartouche of the pharaoh. To anyone but Siptah, the message would be meaningless as nobody at that time would have associated Horemosis with the god Sobek as Horemosis had never even ventured to the Temple of Sobek.

Siptah had died knowing that his secret would be buried with him and that his beloved Horemosis and Hatshepsut would remain forever undisturbed. What he hadn't counted on was his own tomb being desecrated and the papyrus wandering off into other hands that may ultimately unravel his secret.

Over three thousand years later, the tomb of Siptah was found by local grave robbers. It contained little of precious value, which was fenced through a network of antique dealers operating out of Cairo's Khan al Khalili bazaar. The papyrus scroll, although authentic, was not considered very valuable and was eventually purchased by a wealthy English woman on her way by ship to Candy in Ceylon. To avoid any problems with customs inspectors, she concealed the scroll in her first-edition Cook's leather-bound guidebook to Egypt and forgot about it.

The scroll would lay dormant, safely tucked away inside the guidebook in the family library throughout two world wars, and would not be seen again for another eighty years.

CHAPTER 1

Times were very hard, and the workplace had become a painful battlefield for those keen enough to climb the corporate ladder. George Drake was caught right in the middle of this rat race, and like many, he thought there must be a better way to earn a living.

He had moved to South Wales several years earlier having forfeited an army career and an opportunity of obtaining a commission in the Queen's Regiment in Canterbury. After graduating from school he had also experimented living and working in Cambridge in a laboratory, and while he enjoyed the lifestyle in what was a predominantly student environment, he once again felt trapped and unable to progress with what was also a poor career choice.

Now a successful insurance broker he lived and worked in Cardiff for a small provincial firm called Federated Insurance Brokers. It was a pleasant and safe environment, and his coworkers all liked him.

George actually stuck out like a sore thumb as he was a true aristocrat, and although he had no family estate per se, he claimed to be of noble "Stuart blood" and of better lineage than the House of Windsor!

He was six foot tall, and despite having been in a nine-to-five routine for the past ten years had managed to keep in excellent shape. At the age of thirty-five he was now in his prime without an ounce of fat on him. With piercing blue eyes and a thick main of blond hair, everyone was surprised that he had not yet managed to settle down with a steady girlfriend even though he had a long string of admirers.

Glyn Williams, who worked for the same group, did the morning car run, picking up George and two others in his worn-out Fiat 127, music bellowing out from "Jaws," his newly installed Motorola cassette recorder, appropriately named as tapes rarely survived more than a week.

It was a cold winter morning, and George was full of the Monday-morning blues. Glyn had picked George up at 8:30 a.m., joined the rush-hour traffic, and eventually followed a municipal bus into Windsor Place managing to squeeze into a small gap under a row of leafless trees. Traffic wardens regularly patrolled the zone, and Glyn would have to go out and find another place within a couple hours, repeating the process every few hours. It was for this reason that George was happy to get the lift into town and avoid the frustrations of parking tickets.

George eased out of the car and made off for No. 31. He pushed the heavy oak door and climbed up a narrow staircase to his shared office, which was sparsely furnished with three desks. Chris, his boss, was already in and engrossed in reading the *South Wales Echo*. Contemplating this monotonous scene George strode down the corridor into the kitchen and made himself a mug of Earl Grey tea, then returned to his desk, picked up the phone, and dialed Glyn across the road. He was bored with the mundane, nine-to-five, robotic daily routines and knew it was time to quit.

"Hey Glyn, What are you doing for lunch today? I need to talk!"

Glyn suggested a pie and pint down at the Castle Inn at one o'clock.

At 12:30 p.m. George left the office and walked down Windsor Place onto Queen Street, which by now was full of weekday shoppers despite heavy drizzle. The weather was one of a number of factors that made George feel so depressed, the others being lack of excitement and a suitable partner. He was alone and desperate to live his life to the fullest and experience more of an outdoor existence while he was still young and able.

Within fifteen minutes, George reached the Castle Inn, which was just across the road from the Cardiff Castle; it was a cozy spot and was already filling up with its regular lunchtime crowd. Pushing his way through the throng of people, George headed for the bar and ordered a pint of Brains Dark and a cheese-and-pickle sandwich. Glyn arrived ten minutes later and hailed the bartender for another round. George always made sure he arrived first to try and avoid buying too many rounds!

"So, George, what's up with you today? You were quiet in the car and sounded down in the dumps on the phone."

"Yeah, things aren't really going the way I'd always hoped. I live comfortably, have my own place, but I can't go on like this forever. There must be more to life!" George pulled out a holiday brochure titled 18-30s Club. "I think it's time to get my act together."

"What do you mean?"

"I'm bored!" George uncharacteristically threw his arms up and caught the eye of the bartender signaling for another round. He then opened the brochure and pointed at the section on Egypt. "I've always had a fascination for Egypt and thought it would be a good idea to quit my job and take an extended vacation there. Plus, with a bit of luck, I can tag along with a winter archeological dig, which are always going on. As a matter of fact, I've already done some research and contacted the British Museum, who are supporting a number of such expeditions, and asked if I could volunteer my services. I surprisingly received a positive response. The only caveat was that I had to get there at my own expense."

"Are you sure you're feeling okay?" Glyn said. "Did you have too much to drink on Friday at Monte's Disco?"

"No, not really! My brain has been working overtime, and I feel I have to take the plunge and act on instinct. This weekend I intend to drive home to my parents and break the news. I'll ask them to sell the flat, and once and for all I'll be totally independent."

"How soon do you plan to go ahead with this venture?"

"Well, I dropped a note on Chris's desk this morning, formally giving my one-month notice. I suspect I'll be called in to see Sir J, who will wonder what I'm up to and probably attempt to buy me back with a small increment, but my mind is made up, and I'm going to look for something totally new!"

Glyn lit up his fifth cigarette, blew a puff of thick, blue smoke, and pondered over what George had said. He then announced that he thought the idea was outrageous and wished he had the guts to do the same. "Anything I can do to help you get on your way, you can count on me."

Before heading back to the office, they agreed to meet at JJ's house that evening with all the guys, as it was their weekly snooker night, at which point the news could be conveyed to the rest of the gang. JJ was Sir J's son and close friend of George. In fact, it was this friendship that had led George to join the company and move to Cardiff. Having the support of friends like these had made life sustainable, and leaving them would be the hardest part of the whole plan. One consolation, however, was that he would no longer remain indebted to JJ's family and could bond more freely.

The afternoon was uneventful; Chris had clearly read the resignation note and passed it down to Sir J's secretary. He avoided the subject and said Sir J would see him the following morning.

At five o'clock, Glyn honked his horn outside the office window. George rushed out beginning to feel the excitement building up in his body. He joked with Glyn all the way to Llandaff, where his apartment was, and before being dropped off he agreed to meet at JJ's house in Lisvane at 9:00 p.m.

George's apartment was neat and sparkling clean, a trait picked up from his public-school education. He had spent five years at Oundle, which he frequently declared the best years of his life. He was often described by his teachers as a bit of a rebel but was considered by his friends as a leader. He was a keen oarsman and had made the first eight. It was as a result of this activity that his body had developed into a sleek muscle machine, and he kept it up by running several miles each day. He also took an interest in helping the local Llandaff rowing club where he enjoyed coaching an all-female crew, who considered him a bit of a sadist.

Settling down into an easy chair, he opened a can of beer and wondered whether he had made the right decision. His mind wandered, and the thought of what lay ahead reassured him.

Having relaxed for a couple hours, he jumped in the shower, shaved, and got ready for the evening's snooker. Wearing jeans and a T-shirt, George walked down to the garage and pulled up the shutter door. Inside was a 1969 Red MGB Roadster, his pride and joy despite its expensive upkeep. Turning the ignition the engine came to life, its twin carburetors giving a throaty purr. Pulling out he put his foot down on the accelerator and roared across town to the rich suburb of Lisvane. JJ lived in Sir J's old residence, which had sprawling gardens and was probably the most valuable piece of real estate in all of Cardiff. Cars were already parked outside including Glyn's Fiat 127.

George opened the front door and found his way to the snooker room where everyone had assembled. JJ was slouched over the snooker table attempting a difficult shot into the side pocket.

"Hi everyone," George said before maneuvering himself to the bar at the far side of the room.

JJ, having missed his shot, came over and patted him on the shoulder. "I hear your leaving us," he said.

"Yeah, I'm sure Glyn has briefed you regarding my plans, which probably seem a little bizarre."

"You can say that again. I gather you're seeing the old man tomorrow? Knowing him, he's going to try and talk you out of it."

Theresa, one of JJ's longtime friends, came over and joined the conversation with her husband, Rob. Both Rob and Theresa had been among George's closest friends while he had been in Cardiff, and it was Rob who was a keen MG enthusiast and had found George his current vehicle. George's brother, Bill, a chartered accountant and JJ's best friend, came over with "Taffy," a bouncer. Bill was unimpressed with George's plan and said he was mad. There was not a lot of love lost between these two, particularly after Bill had locked George out of his apartment during a party and had left him to throw up over his neighbor's doorstep. The police were called, and he nearly got arrested for being drunk and disorderly.

"Well," said George, "at least this plan of mine will get me out of your hair, not to mention no more free Sunday lunches for you!"

Bill moved away. Everyone else supported George, and opposing the venture would serve no real purpose. Theresa pulled George over and asked him how he was going to get to the site in Egypt and how long he would stick it out.

"I booked a flight to Luxor and will be meeting up with a Doctor Hugh Randall of the British Museum at the Hilton. The whole team is apparently staying there and will let me bunk with them on arrival. As for how long I might stick it out, that depends on how things go and is completely open." George asked Theresa if Rob would look after his MG while he was away, and she agreed that he would love to and promised she would make him take good care of it.

George then shot a few frames of snooker, beating everyone, and declared it was time to head out. He was careful not to drink too much and drove home.

The following morning, George was summoned to the inner sanctum of Sir J to explain his sudden wish to leave the firm. Sir J, now well into his eighties, had had an impressive career. He was a self-made millionaire who had a remarkable eye for deals. His current operations included his own bank, finance company, and the small insurance brokerage George had been a part of these past ten years.

"So, George, I've received your note, and before accepting what you have to say, I wonder whether I can interest you in staying with us. JJ's now on the board and is keen to see you promoted."

George explained that the job had nothing to do with his decision and that it was something he just had to do.

"Okay," said Sir J, "what I'll do is keep your job open for you for a month just in case you change your mind. I know all too well we sometimes make irrational decisions and need time away to reflect on our choices."

This was indeed a welcome compromise and would make life a lot easier for him when breaking the news to his parents this weekend.

"Thanks, Sir J. You don't know what this means to me, as well as having your support, which I value dearly."

"As you may not be aware, I've always been a supporter for those who go it alone as I did fifty years ago. I'm also a benefactor of the British Museum and support projects such as the one you're embarking on, so do please keep us posted, and let us know how you're getting on. I wish you all the best on your adventure."

CHAPTER 2

Friday afternoon came surprisingly quickly; George had not spoken further on the subject and had quietly kept to himself. News of Sir J's generosity had leaked out, and many in the office were noticeably jealous of the special relationship between George and Sir J.

George drove to the office in his MG and parked in a nearby multistory garage. As he had made arrangements to visit his parents in Shrewsbury and wanted to get there in daylight, if possible, he asked Chris if he could leave early and make it up next week. Although he was now leaving the firm, such an offer was more of a courteous gesture. The drive home was one he regularly undertook and passed through some beautiful countryside. Wishing everyone a pleasant weekend, he left the office at three clock and motored down the M4 toward Symonds Yat. He then turned off and headed north past Ross on Wye through Church Stretton into Shrewsbury.

The Drakes lived in an old-listed house called the Grange just outside Meole Village. It was still the largest property in the area, and half of it was unoccupied. George loved this house and always remembered the good times he had had with his sister and three brothers. His father, Fred, was a World War II veteran of the Burma campaign who had made his fortune resurrecting the family tile business. Retired now, he always maintained an active interest in the children's welfare, hence the odd hand out when they were ever in difficulty. His mother came from a wealthy Dutch family, and the mix had clearly worked well for George who was by far the most dashing of their offspring, not to mention the most troublesome.

Pulling into the driveway past ancient white gates, rotten with age, George saw the Grange and slowly moved his MG in a large semicircle and parked opposite the front door. The porch was impressive and had been designed for visitors arriving by horse and carriage. Moving to the door, George pulled the old-fashioned chain and heard a clang as the bell chimed in the hall beyond as he knew the heavy oak door would be bolted from inside . Hearing the cast-iron bolt moved into position, Elizabeth, his mother opened the door and gave him a big hug.

"It's so nice to see you. You don't come to see us enough! And why didn't you use the back door? You know we always leave it open during the day," she complained, although she was happy that her youngest was back home. "I've made your old room up, and your father's in the lounge waiting for you." Bill must have spilled the beans and told them what was going on.

Putting down his small overnight bag, George strode into the living room, where his father was seated in his usual chair with a scotch in one hand and newspaper in the other. He had a passion for doing the *Telegraph* puzzle and had an array of reference books by his side.

Registering George's arrival, he got up and greeted him. "So, George, I'm glad you came up this weekend as I've been hearing some odd rumors about you resigning and taking an extended vacation. Tell me it's not true?"

George headed for the drink cabinet and decided to fix himself a stiff G&T before answering the question. Nervously opening the two mahogany doors, he took a bohemian crystal glass, poured in a large measure of gin, and fumbled with the ice and lemon. He then took a Schweppes tonic and added a drop of angostura bitter as a finishing touch.

"Dad, I'm not going to beat around the bush; yes, it's all true. I handed in my resignation last week. However, you'll be pleased to note that Sir J, while accepting my position, is keeping my job open for a short while in case I change my mind." Before his father could interject, George added, "This decision has come after a great deal of thought, and nothing you say is going to stop me from going ahead with it." Gulping back his drink, he waited for an angry response. However, much to his surprise, his father sat down and said he would support whatever decision George made and only hoped he would find what he was looking for so he could settle down and live a normal life.

Elizabeth Drake was not so happy. She worried that something bad might happen and that they would have no way of knowing what was going on. George reassured her that he would write regularly and call whenever possible.

George then sat down and discussed all the latest gossip from Cardiff and listened to news about the rest of the family.

He slept well that night, and the following morning George sat down with Fred and talked over the sale of his apartment, which would be put into the hands of local real-estate agents the next week. As the apartment was located in one of the nicer parts of Cardiff, it wouldn't take too long to sell, and a reasonable profit was sure to materialize.

That afternoon George rummaged through the room under the stairs where there was a considerable amount of archive material on Egypt collected by his great-aunt Conti who had traveled there at the turn of the century. As a child he had often looked through her handwritten journals and faded photographs, which had sparked his initial interest in Egyptian history.

The box room was full of junk accumulated since the war when the family had first moved to Shrewsbury. Having sifted through about twenty large boxes, George finally found his great-aunt's box. Apart from the journals and pictures of numerous monuments and temples that documented her passage through the Suez Canal, he came across a tattered first-edition guidebook that contained detailed maps of all the major archeological sites among other tourist information. The leather-bound book was dated 1901 and had no reference to Tutankhamun, who at that time had not yet been discovered.

George took the box out and headed for the sunroom where the atmosphere was more pleasant. Something told him that the material contained in this box could prove invaluable for him on the forthcoming expedition. He decided to go through every page of the guidebook with a fine-tooth comb, as he knew his eccentric great-aunt had a habit of hiding clues.

After several hours of reading what was very small print, nothing of interest had turned up; however, with the sunlight now shining on the coarse leather binding, George noticed that the right-hand side of the book had been repaired or restitched. With his curiosity mounting he dug into his pocket and took out his Swiss Army knife (an item he always carried), and carefully cut open the stitches. The opening didn't damage the book but revealed a gap between the leather and cardboard infill. Within this gap he found a piece of parchment made from papyrus. George's heart began to beat faster as pulled it free and turned it over. On it were a number of hieroglyphics and a map, all of which was completely mysterious to him.

George now knew that his decision to go to Egypt was one of destiny.

The map was clearly a valuable document, and its content would have to remain secret. With this in mind George put the map back inside the book, went up to his room, and packed the book into his overnight bag.

Once he got back to Cardiff, he decided that he would copy the hieroglyphics, and since he was not really needed in the office, he would take a train to London and see the curator of the Egyptian section of the British Museum. Hopefully they would be able to shed some light on this find, although he would not reveal the source from where they had come.

The two days in Shrewsbury had completely revitalized George, and with the winter sun still shining and giving some warmth, George had the top down on his MG and waved goodbye as he rolled out through the main gates.

CHAPTER 3

All the way back to Cardiff, George couldn't stop thinking about his find and how he was going to investigate the contents. Sunday-afternoon traffic was light, and within two hours he was already parking the MG in his garage port. Once in his apartment, he turned up the heat and pulled a cold beer from the fridge.

Having secured the original manuscript from prying eyes, George decided to turn in, in order to get an early start the next morning. He had already made up his mind that work was out of the question, and he would instead head straight for Cardiff Central Station and catch the "Brain Train" to London Paddington.

Drifting off to sleep, he longed for his final departure to Egypt and the unknown.

At 5:30 a.m., George was wide awake. His morning routine had not changed since he had left Oundle. Breakfast consisted of a sacred bowl of cereal topped with full-cream milk accompanied by a steaming hot cup of traditional English breakfast tea. Having downed this in less than five minutes, he then had a quick shower and shave and called for a radio taxi to pick him up in an hour.

Just before exiting the apartment, George called JJ to apologize for his absence from the office and asked if he would let Chris know. JJ told George not to worry and that they would consider his resignation with immediate effect.

Putting down the receiver, George rushed out the door to meet the waiting taxi, double-checking that he had his copy of the manuscript.

The driver must have been at the end of his shift and grumbled all the way to Cardiff Central. The cab was filthy and wreaked of stale cigarettes. Once at the station George made for the ticket counter, purchasing an open return to Paddington.

George climbed the old stone stairs to Platform 2 and waited for the high-speed inter-city train to arrive. Soon a high-pitched hoot in the distance indicated it was just around the corner, so George decided to purchase a morning newspaper to give him something to read. Fortunately the high-pressure weather front had held, and while the air was brisk with plumes of vapor streaming out of rosy faces, the sun was shining, and for Cardiff, this was heaven.

The train whined down the platform with mundane precision. Doors clanked as passengers disembarked and guards sounded out "Cardiff Central! All aboard for London Paddington!"

George parked himself in a second-class seat near the restaurant car in the no-smoking section and watched the other passengers as they settled down. Trains were always fascinating places to see people from all different walks of life. He hoped a sexy-looking girl would sit next to him; however, this would not be the case, and to his horror, he had to put up with a small group of skinheads who were obviously off to the city to cause trouble.

He immersed himself in his newspaper to avoid catching their attention, and as soon as the train started moving, decided to treat himself to a second breakfast in the restaurant car, if not only to get away from this gang of undesirables.

George loved eating on trains and remembered when he was a child traveling on the old steam engines from Shrewsbury to London Euston. The modern Pullman coaches were no match for the old classics, though it was still pleasant and a good way to break the monotonous journey

The "Brain Train" mainly catered to business passengers who reached the city before 9:00 a.m., allowing a full day's work. It only made two stops, one at Bristol Parkway and the second at Reading. By 8:50 a.m., it had begun to slow down and screeched a clear sign that Paddington was only five minutes away. George had managed to finish his breakfast with a few cups of tea. He walked over to one of the doors, opened the window, and peered out to see where they were. The cool air rushed against his face, reinvigorating him. Paddington inched closer, and inside the terminal, thousands of people could be seen filing out of trains toward the underground, ground transport, and to other platforms. Announcements of different departures bellowed from the PA system. Even before the train came to a standstill other doors opened, and people jumped off to get a thirty-second head start. George decided to follow suit rather than get caught in the bedlam and jumped to the platform. He then briskly walked to the nearest underground map and checked which route to take. Unfortunately he would have to make a change to get on to the central line, and at this time of day it was better than taking a taxi.

George slipped the correct change into a ticket vending machine, collected the ticket, and joined the mass of people down to the westbound platform of the Circle Line.

The underground was another favorite observation post for George. Everyone looked so defensive and tended to avoid eye contact. Many stood with books open and made themselves appear to be reading, although it was probably far too difficult to concentrate with all the activity and commotion.

George decided to get off at Holborn and walk to the British Museum. He remembered Holborn well as following Oundle he had commuted from Cambridge to London for three months working at No. 1 Drury Lane while employed by Spillers Grain & Feed. How boring that had been, but what an excellent learning experience. He often wondered how graduates today would ever find a suitable job. Experimenting with different jobs was necessary and could take a few years to find the right fit. George had gone straight from school to work in a laboratory with Spillers. From there he did a spell with the Queen's Regiment in Kent and attended Regular Commissions Board before finally working for Sir J. Within that time he had also been interviewed and accepted to become an inspector in the Royal Hong Kong Police. How he ended up as an insurance broker was still beyond his comprehension and, rightly or wrongly, was driven by a preference to take the safe route rather than venturing out of his comfort zone. That had all changed now as his father's words of advice reverberated in his brain: "If there's no risk in life, then life's a bore."

Holborn was deep underground, and the climb up the old wooden escalators offered good exercise. George was in the mood and keen to get to the museum as quickly as possible.

On surfacing and passing through the exit turnstile, he walked out into the street and headed toward Tottenham Court Road. He eventually got his bearings and found the museum after half an hour of brisk walking.

The Egyptian collection was on the right side and occupied an enormous area. George made for the information desk and asked for the curator, having already set up the meeting in advance of his trip to London in order to discuss his curious find.

Professor Alistair Johnston, the museum's Egyptian artefacts specialist, had agreed to meet George for a few minutes to hear what this find was all about and sent a secretary to guide him into the depths of the building. Passing through a door marked Private, they moved to an old elevator with Meccano-like gates. This took them three floors down into the basement. Clearly there were treasures hidden here which probably outnumbered those on display.

The secretary parked George in a small annex and waddled off to alert Professor Johnston. Some minutes later, George heard heavy footsteps approaching. Alistair Johnston pushed the door making it slam into the wall and stood in the doorway as if he were in a Western movie. Surprisingly he was younger than George had expected, possibly in his midforties with tough Arian features, although he had obviously overindulged with too many heavy business lunches.

"Well, Mr. Drake, what do you have to show me?"

George pulled out the copy of the manuscript and explained how he had come across it.

"How do you know it's an original and not a fake?" Johnston barked.

"I don't think my great-aunt would have gone to such lengths to conceal the document in her guidebook at that time unless it had some value and was an original antiquity," George replied somewhat defensively.

Johnston scowled and took the document. "Do you mind if I get these hieroglyphics translated? Perhaps you'd like to wait here for a short while? It will only take my team a few minutes to decipher the main points."

Before George could even respond, Johnston took off. George sat down and began to wonder whether he had made the right decision by coming to the museum.

Ten minutes later, Johnston appeared again. His expression had changed. He now had a notepad with him and was closely followed by a young assistant who George concluded was Egyptian. George was hypnotized by her startling beauty.

Johnston sat down and started firing questions while fiddling with his ballpoint pen. He then wanted to know more about where the manuscript was originally located.

Having been interrogated for over half an hour, George stood and said, "Okay, you've had your turn, now let me ask you what all this is about. My manuscript is obviously of interest, why? What does it say?"

The assistant spoke. She had a slightly husky but sexy voice. Her name was Sherifa, and she was on assignment in London, on loan from the Ministry of Antiquities. Her area of specialization was in the interpretation of ancient scripts, including hieroglyphics.

"Mr. Drake, these are very interesting symbols, and I'd assume the parchment, if it's genuine, is dated somewhere between the seventeenth and eighteenth dynastic period within the New Kingdom, as it makes reference to a funeral of a great king and his final journey to the afterlife. However, his name isn't one we've come across and could alter the lineage history as we understand it."

Johnston looked at her angrily as if she was divulging too much information.

"Will it be possible for you to return here with the original scroll and also bring along the guidebook so we can see if your great-aunt made any reference to it in the book? It will also give me an opportunity to run some tests on the parchment to get an exact date and let you know if what you have is authentic or just a fake."

George mulled it over and said he would consider it. In the meantime, he wanted to confirm his position on the Luxor excavation and was aiming to join the team within the next few weeks. Johnston seemed to get even more agitated at the mention of this and stormed out.

"What's wrong with him?" George said.

Sherifa came closer to George. "I don't think you realize what you may have if the document is real. Apart from the papyrus having some value, what it can actually tell us may be far more valuable."

"This is bigger than I thought! Johnston seems to want to lay his hands on it and take any credit if there is indeed something locked inside. What do you suggest I do?"

"Look, this is exciting for me too. The only way you'll get a proper answer is to bring the original to London so we can examine it closer."

Feeling the beginning of a connection, and that Sherifa was on his side, George gambled and asked Sherifa if she wanted to get a coffee. To his surprise, she accepted.

Finding their way back up to the main level, they walked outside and across the road to a small sandwich bar where they found a quiet table. Breaking the ice, George asked Sherifa for her order and instructed the waiter to bring two cafe au laits.

George said, "Well, tell me, what do you think?"

"I don't know how to put it. You have something that should really belong to Egypt, which is why I agreed to come out here, because I don't want you to pass it on to Johnston."

"What do you mean?"

"The papyrus, it seems, might help guide us to a royal tomb as yet undiscovered. The reason I say *undiscovered* is because many of the symbols detailed in your drawings have never been seen before and depict the pharaoh at the time taking a ship up into the heavens. As it relates to the New Kingdom, we'll be sure to unlock the secrets of this papyrus in the Valley of the Kings, where all the royals were buried. Needless to say, if this tomb has never been discovered, it's very likely still intact and possibly the discovery of the century. That's why Johnston was behaving that way." She sighed. "Since I arrived here three months ago, I've noticed that Johnston can be quite ruthless. Since you contacted the British Museum to meet up with one of their excavation teams, he knows you're going to Luxor and will probably have you closely watched now that he knows what you possess."

"I think I'd better stay out of his way for the time being. Maybe he'll forget about it? After all, he does have a copy of the papyrus."

"No! What you gave us today isn't enough. Was there any more writing on the original? There may also be other clues that you haven't found yet in the book, as Johnston suggested. After all, you did say your great-aunt had an eye for detail, right?"

"Hmmm, I hadn't thought about that. When I get back home, I'll take a closer look at it, particularly with regard to the section on the New Kingdom and the Valley of the Kings. Tell me, Sherifa, when are you going back to Cairo? Would you mind giving me your phone number so I can call you when I get back and let you know what's happening?"

Sherifa pulled out a packet of Cartier cigarettes and expertly flicked a zippo lighter into action. She then retrieved a pen from her bag and jotted her number on a napkin and handed it to George. Her soft hands brushed against George's arm and sent a tingle down his spine.

With the business side concluded, they changed the subject and talked about their pasts over another coffee. After an hour, Sherifa said she had better get back to the museum, otherwise they would wonder where she was. George walked her back, and just before saying goodbye, he took her hand and kissed it. Sherifa smiled and thought George was just the sort of guy she would like to get to know better if such an opportunity arose.

Turning away, George strolled back to Tottenham Court Road and made for the underground on the corner by Center Point. It was only midday; however, he had nothing more to do and decided to return to Paddington and catch the next train back to Cardiff.

George made good time and with a bit of luck managed to board the one o'clock train. He wasn't hungry but instead stood at the bar and chatted with the bartender over a couple beers. He then sat down and thought about Sherifa and when he would see her again. The beers made him feel drowsy, and he dozed off for half an hour before being awoken by the conductor checking tickets. Twenty minutes later the train arrived at Cardiff Central.

George realized something was wrong the moment his taxi edged around the corner of Llandaff Road and spotted a police car outside his block of apartments, blue lights flashing and his neighbor, Mrs. Evans, looking extremely worried.

As the taxi came to a stop, George got out. Mrs. Evans rushed over. "Oh, Mr. Drake, I'm so sorry. I didn't realize you were away and called the police as I saw two men rummaging through your apartment.

They must have seen me and left just before the police got here."

George thanked Mrs. Evans and rushed up the stairs to assess the damage. Inside the apartment he found a couple of police officers investigating the crime scene as everything had been turned upside down.

Inspector Gordon Davies from the local Llandaff police station came over and asked George if anything was missing, a question he thought inappropriate since he had only just stepped through the door. Quickly surveying the living room, George concluded that everything appeared in place, which puzzled the police who were now short of a motive for the burglary and more suspicious about George. What had they been after?

As there was no physical damage, Inspector Davies suggested George make a list of any items missing and come to the station in the morning to provide some details for the official report. George agreed. Inspector Davies left, leaving George to tidy up the mess.

Once the apartment was clear, George, headed for the airing cupboard to check for the guidebook. Fortunately, it was still in place having been expertly concealed. Johnston had certainly not wasted any time. George decided it was time to wrap up all outstanding matters and get on his way to Egypt as quickly as possible.

He started cleaning up the mess and wondered whether the goons that had broken in would try again. Hopefully, the fact that the police had gotten to the scene so quickly would make them think twice.

Once everything was back in place, George dialed the number Sherifa had given him.

"Oh, I'm so glad you called," she said when she answered. "I haven't been able to stop thinking about you, and that's not a good sign."

"Well, things have been quite hot up here," George said, then he recounted the story of the burglary.

"George, please be careful. I told you Johnston was ruthless, and this proves my point. I don't want to see you get hurt!"

"Now don't you worry. I'm going to lay low for a while and will let you know when I plan to leave for Cairo."

CHAPTER 4

The next morning, George called the movers to pack up his belongings and have them transported to the Grange. He also called the estate agents and had the property put on the market, giving his parents' address as their point of contact. The only items he kept for himself was a small backpack with a few changes of clothes and his precious first-edition guidebook.

While the movers were at work, he took out the MG and paid a visit to Inspector Davies at the station. When George told him he was moving out, an air of suspicion obviously crossed Davies's mind.

"Was it the burglary?" Davies asked.

"No, I'd been planning this move for some time now and decided to bring it to a head. Incidentally, I came over to let you know that nothing was missing and that the quick action of Mrs. Evans must have saved the day."

Davies thanked him for his cooperation and wished him luck on his journey.

George left the station and drove off to Rob and Theresa's place. As Theresa opened the door, he announced that the time had come for him to leave his baby at their house, knowing that it would be well looked after in his absence. Theresa dragged George in and made him a cup of tea. Ziggy, their cat, tried to attack his feet as she was always excited when visitors arrived.

George handed the keys to Theresa and said that the MOT and Insurance were all up to date and that she needn't worry about anything. "Please keep track of any bills and I'll pay you back," reminded George. He then asked if he could use the phone and made two calls, one to organize another taxi to the station and the other to Sherifa to tell her he was on his way back to London. Sherifa suggested they meet at the Sherlock Holmes Pub just off Trafalgar Square in Old Scotland Yard. George agreed and said he would be there at 7:00 p.m.

George decided it was best not to involve any of the family with his find, as the less they knew the better. When the taxi finally arrived, he gave Theresa a big hug and asked her to tell his brother and all the lads that he was on his way to Cairo.

He arrived back in London in plenty of time and found his way to Trafalgar Square where, to kill time, he bought some food for the pigeons and joined a gathering of tourists beneath Nelson's Column and the bronze lions. As soon as he had the cup in his hand, birds from all directions mobbed him. The municipality was much more organized these days, and every few hours they hosed down the square to keep it from getting spoiled.

At 6:30 p.m. he crossed the road and walked down toward the Victoria Embankment and found the Sherlock Holmes nestled on the corner of Old Scotland Yard.

Sherifa, who said she preferred being called Sherry for short, arrived right on time. Her apartment was only a few minutes away, situated just behind the old war office off Horse Guards Parade. George ordered another pint of Fuller's Bitter and a tequila sunrise for Sherry. He handed over the orange-and-red concoction, and Sherry thanked him. She lifted up the umbrella cocktail stick and enticingly bit into the glazed cherry that decorated the drink.

"Hmm, thank you, George. This is a nice change for me as I don't go out much, and I rarely meet people in the museum since I'm hidden away in the basement."

"This is a pleasure for me too as you can see from the looks of all the guys who are thinking how lucky I am to be in the company of such a beautiful woman," George beamed.

"Well, that makes two of us since you're certainly the most handsome man in this establishment!"

George then went over the day's events and concluded he was ready to leave for Cairo.

"Do you have a visa for Egypt? While you can get one at the airport, it's better to get the paperwork sorted out in advance. Since I work for a division of the government, I can help you get this sorted through the embassy here and get the museum to provide a letter of introduction."

After they finished their drinks, George took Sherry's hand and walked her down to the embankment. As they walked he pulled her gently toward him and asked if it would be all right to kiss her. Sherry consented and met his lips with a degree of passion that sent a shot of adrenaline into George's system. She felt the excitement between his legs and broke away blushing.

They walked back to the apartment hand in hand, and once inside, Sherry showed George the spare room so he wouldn't get the wrong idea.

With Sherry's help, the process of obtaining the visa for Egypt was painless. Within half an hour of walking into the embassy, he had the official stamp in his passport with a special three-month extension, sufficient to see him through to the end of the digging season.

Sherry left for the museum afterward and arranged to catch up with George that evening.

George walked down Hyde Park to Marble Arch and into Thomas Cook's office to make reservations for his flight. BA had a daily flight to Cairo, and in order to tie up any loose ends, he decided to fix his departure for the following week. While he had his credit card, he also purchased a thousand pounds' worth of traveler's checks along with some local currency. Fortunately he had plenty funds in his account to keep him self-sufficient for several months without having to worry too much about cash flow, and with the cost of living in Egypt being substantially lower he felt even more relaxed. George then picked up two tickets to *Phantom of the Opera* and booked a table at a small Italian restaurant just around the corner from the Shaftsbury Theatre where it was showing.

When they finally met by the statue of William Shakespeare in Leicester Square Sherry was delighted when she heard the evening's plans and hugged George. "Wow, what a surprise! You really are giving me the royal treatment tonight," Sherry said.

Soon they reached the restaurant and sat down outside next to a decorative gas heater that generated a welcome warmth to the overall ambience and strengthened the magnetic attraction building up between them.

"You deserve far more, as without your intervention at the museum I'd probably be on a completely different path. So this is really a thank you, not to mention that I hope to get to know you better," George replied.

Just then a lady passed through the restaurant selling individually wrapped red roses. George hailed her over to their table and bought one and handed it to Sherry.

"What a fortuitous coincidence. I couldn't have planned it better. Thank you again!"

Sherry was completely bowled over having never been treated this way before. George was a true gentleman.

The dinner was superb, washed down with a fine bottle of Brown Brothers chardonnay and their first opportunity to sit together in relaxed surroundings and really enjoy each other's company. There was no further talk of the forthcoming trip or work at the museum. After dinner, they strolled over to the theater, found their seats, and managed to book a half bottle of champagne for the interval. The music and dance was brilliant, and at the close, George noticed a few tears trickling slowly down Sherry's cheeks.

Managing to flag a cab after the performance was a real problem; however, they eventually succeeded. Sneaking back into the apartment in the early hours, they decided to end the perfect evening with a coffee and Cointreau.

Sherry nestled in close to George, and with the liquor now warming her she put down her glass and moved toward George. The electricity of the connection was mind-blowing, and not wanting to be too presumptuous, George decided it was best to call it a day and head to the spare room Sherry had prepared for his stay.

As they parted company, Sherry kissed him again, thanking him for a wonderful evening.

"You really have given me a fresh perspective about the English, as we Egyptians tend to steer well away from them. You're one in a million!" Sherry blew a final kiss as she turned and headed to her own room.

George awoke at daybreak thinking of how wonderful their evening had been.

After his shower, he made a pot of coffee for Sherry and brought her a mug in bed. She sighed with delight as he passed her the mug and propped herself on an elbow, so she could drink the coffee without spilling it.

With only a few days to go before departure, George suggested they take a look at the original papyrus after breakfast to see if they could decipher any more messages. At the mention of this, Sherry jumped out of bed with excitement. This would be the first time that she would have an opportunity to view the original scroll. Even the hot coffee that had splashed over her thigh was not enough to squelch her enthusiasm.

George had already pulled out the old guidebook and carefully removed the papyrus placing it on the kitchen table under an illuminated magnifying glass.

Sherry sat down on a stool and nuzzled next to George. Looking though the bulbous glass loupe, the colored pictures began to unfold their secrets that had been locked in time for over three thousand years.

What George had originally copied and passed on to Johnston was only the central diagram, picturing the young pharaoh making his final journey, crossing over from the living into the arms of Anubis and taking his place in the City of the Dead.

Sherry was able to decipher the surrounding hieroglyphics and slowly unfold the mystery that had been so aptly kept from prying eyes. It was clearly some form of map, as beneath the characters were further instructions guiding the reader to what appeared to be another ancient-Egyptian god named "Sobek." Continuing her interpretation and breaking what appeared to be a deafening silence, she said, "Fifty paces down some form of passage leading to the Place of Crocodiles you will find a spot marked by the cartouche of the young pharaoh. It seems almost too easy! Your great-aunt, of course, picked up the papyrus at a time when hieroglyphics weren't really understood. Had it not been hidden all this time, the secret behind our unidentified pharaoh's cartouche would have already been solved! We're holding on to something so valuable it's not only unbelievable, but it's frightening."

George was excited and nodded for her to go on.

"Do you know, the only place I can think of dedicated to Sobek and where crocodiles would have been present would be the Temple of Kom Ombo. Many people think this temple was built post-New Kingdom at the time of the Ptolemies; however, if I'm right, and Kom Ombo is the answer, then clearly its history goes much further back. But we won't need to worry about crocodiles anymore, since Gamal Abdul Nasser built the High Dam at Aswan, all the crocs have disappeared and can only be found on the other side of the dam."

"Did you just say *we?*" George said.

"Naturally, do you think I can stay here knowing what I do now? Johnston must have figured out by now that you've shown me the full manuscript and that if there were something of value in it, I would have found it. That's why I said it's so frightening. We've stumbled onto a gold mine, and the likes of Johnston will do anything to get his hands on it."

"My god, Sherry, you really do think the worst! Although, you know him better than I do, and judging from my previous experience in Cardiff, I think you may be right. Since we know what we're looking for, I suggest we mail the original scroll to my parents' house in Shrewsbury. They'll secure it in the family safe-deposit box out of harm's way at Lloyds Bank, as Johnston is sure to think we'll keep the document with us for future reference."

Sherry scribbled down a few notes in her diary as George grabbed a strong manila envelope from her desk. He quickly penned down the Grange address in black felt tip, and on the back of the envelope he scribbled a short note: *Dad, can you keep this in the family box at 1 Pride Hill?* The message was short enough not to raise any questions, and he knew it would soon be forgotten about. It was better to ensure his parents knew nothing about the scroll, just in case Johnston did try to dig a little deeper into his past.

Satisfied that everything was now secure George suggested they grab what they needed and leave. "Let's travel in jeans and T-shirts and just take jackets to keep ourselves warm. This way anyone watching won't assume we're leaving the country."

Grabbing a small shoulder bag, Sherry put her few essentials in and made one quick check around her apartment. On the table she left a small note for the cleaning lady to say she would be away for a few days and to shut everything off until she returned.

As they left the apartment building and strolled over toward a bright-red mailbox located on the corner of the street, George noticed a black van pull round the corner of Whitehall Place. It edged slowly forward and in their general direction as if en route to Victoria Embankment station. Reacting instinctively to this rather threatening movement, George jumped out into the street and managed to flag down a passing white hackney cab, blazoned with advertisements for a new West End musical production by Andrew Lloyd Webber.

Pushing Sherry into the back seat, he hopped in alongside and screamed at the driver to put his foot on the peddle and head down Embankment as fast as possible. To make it worth his while, George slipped him twenty quid and said it was a matter of life or death. Charged with an air of urgency, the driver slipped his vehicle through a set of traffic lights just as they were changing back to red, trapping the mysterious black van behind a small pickup. As the taxi sped away and turned off onto Lower Thames Street, the van accelerated into the pickup in front of him pushing it onto the other side of the road and into oncoming traffic. There was a deafening bang as a VW Beetle crashed into the pickup sending debris everywhere. The van continued on in hot pursuit of the taxi.

George bit his thumb nervously, and as they edged around the corner opposite the Tower of London he decided it was best to make off on foot. A red light just above the door handle indicated the door was locked, so George tapped on the glass partition and asked the driver to release the lock and slow down so they could hop out while on the move. The van was still out of site as George pulled the door lever and leapt out pulling Sherry behind him. As his foot hit the ground, George lost his balance and collapsed in a heap grazing his shin. Sherry was more fortunate and had George's body as a buffer between her and the pavement. The fall couldn't have come at a worse time as the van was now in clear view, and the two goons inside had spotted the commotion.

"Dammit," cursed George.

"What's going on!?" Sherry said.

"There are a couple nasty-looking characters on our tail. They've been on to us since we left the flat."

They ran up the narrow path leading to the public entrance of the tower where a crowd of tourists was already milling outside the ticket office. Much to everyone's annoyance, George aggressively pushed to the front of the line and managed to secure two tickets.

Meanwhile, the two goons had abandoned their van and were in hot pursuit up the path.

CHAPTER 5

The two men were ruthless characters who had been hired by Johnston to acquire the papyrus from George by whatever means necessary. The bungled burglary attempt in Cardiff had only fueled their annoyance, and they were now more determined than ever to succeed.

They were an ugly pair. Robin Beaver, the head honcho and staunch Londoner, had barely just stepped out from the gates of Wormwood Scrubs when he had a chance run in with Geoff Harman at a seedy strip club deep in Soho's red-light district. Beaver had curly cropped hair and a pockmarked face, which also bore a number of scars from a series of knife fights that had started from the tender age of eight. He was not a person to mess around with and had been in and out of institutional correction centers for the past twenty years. Making conversation with Beaver was like talking to a brick wall; his eyes would never make contact and instead would roll back and forth from ceiling to floor with his head angled to one side or the other. His demeanor was one of deceit, as if he didn't care for anyone except himself.

Johnston had also happened to be in the club that night sipping a gin and tonic. He was perched in front of the stage eyeing one of the strippers as the burley cockney grabbed the chair next to him. Beaver, with his aggressive manner, knocked over a pint of lager all over Harman, who was slumped in chair next to Johnston.

Harman, no master of the Queen's English, screamed out, "Who the fuck do you think you are, you stupid git!" He had wiped the beer froth from his closely cropped Hitler moustache with the back of his grubby paw. Like Beaver he was a short, stocky guy with a beer belly and tree-trunk neck. While his face was not so marred through teenage combat, he still had a bad case of acne that had been aggravated by his greasy complexion and further exacerbated by a hefty consumption of fast food, smoking cheap cigarettes, and excessive binges in sleazy bars.

Lacking a thirst for aggression, Harman was a typical cockney con man who could easily offload almost any product to ignorant passersby. One of his many jobs was the master of sales at a pawnshop on Oxford Street where he had a knack of luring passing shoppers into the store to dispose of cheap-imitation electronics that were worth only a fraction of the sale price.

At the strip club, Beaver, quick as lightning, had jumped over the stool and grabbed Harman by the throat with one hand and with the other snatched Harman's arm and secured it into a punishing lock. Harman had buckled with a whimpering sob. However, so as not to lose favor with the crowd, which had hovered all around them, he had patted Beaver on the shoulder and said, "Nice move. You caught me by fuckin' surprise, mate! Can I buy you a pint?"

Beaver had simmered down delighted at the prospect of a free drink and joined him at the table. While guzzling down the amber liquid, he had recounted his misfortunes that eventually led him to jail and how he had just come out on parole.

Johnston had overheard the conversation and decided to join in. He slipped a fiver into the shoe of the girl parading herself in front of him and pulled up a stool between the two thugs.

"I hope you don't mind me joining you, but I think I may have a job for you that's right up your alley."

"How the fuck would you know what our alley is?" Harman had blurted, spitting out a mixture of beer and peanuts that had been swirling inside his halitosis-ridden maw.

"There's no need to get excited over this. What I'm trying to say is that I'd like to hire your services, and if you're as good as you seem, I'll make it well worth your while."

"Okay, you've got our attention," Beaver had retorted.

"Right, let me start from the beginning." Johnston had gone on to describe his encounter with Drake and how Drake had somehow managed to get ahold of a valuable manuscript. He doubted that Drake would have any form of security at his apartment in Cardiff and that the document in question would be an easy steal. When he had finished lecturing the two on his planned caper he had described what the document actually looked like. "While you can probably do this tomorrow, if the two of you left for Cardiff on the next train from Paddington you would easily have a two-hour advantage."

Beaver, being a little strapped for cash, had said, "Since this scrap of paper is so valuable, we're going to need five hundred up front to cover expenses, and if we get it, we'll take another ten grand."

Johnston had argued over the final price; however, he had eventually conceded at eight thousand pounds after some souk-style bargaining.

The thugs had made straight for Paddington and boarded the next train for Cardiff. Johnston, having paid them the deposit in cash, had also passed on Drake's address and told them not to be too destructive in their attempt to locate the manuscript and to just try to make it look like a petty burglary.

The trip had proven to be a major disappointment, as neither of them had thought Drake would ever have had the foresight to hide the scroll on top of his water tank. To add to their problems, the nosy next-door neighbor had felt something was off and called the police. Had it not been for the early warning siren, they would have been caught red-handed. However, they had just managed to rush down the stairs, through the back entrance into the garage area, and jumped over a short fence into some garden allotments.

Beaver had cursed their bad luck and decided it would be better to return to the city.

The following morning Johnston, who had heard their news, was furious and summoned them over to his office at the museum.

"I thought you guys were professionals!" Johnston had barked.

"Look here, mate, you obviously underestimated the intelligence of your quarry!" Harman had rebuffed.

"By bringing you a sketch of the parchment, he must have already figured out it had some value and put it in a secure place. We're dealing with someone who has common sense, and getting the document isn't going to be as easy as you might have thought. If we're going to carry on with this, it's going to cost you more as we may need to scare Drake out into the open."

Beaver had grunted in agreement, as the risk of being caught conducting felonious activities was certainly worth more than what had been tabled so far.

Johnston's face had turned crimson as his blood pressure had increased at the prospect of being duped by the two criminals. Such was his desperation to get ahold of the scroll that he had finally conceded and drew up temporary employment contracts for both men.

Beaver had guessed their best bet would be to keep a watch on the Egyptian assistant as Drake would need her as an ally and would ultimately show up again in the city. They had agreed to monitor her apartment, and when the time was right they would make a play for the scroll. Beaver had also managed to get ahold of a gun through his connections with the underworld, which he had intended to use to threaten Drake into releasing the manuscript.

Surveillance of the girl's apartment had been relatively easy, as it was located right next to the Horse Guards Thistle Hotel. The two men had checked in at Johnston's expense using phony identities. Armed with plenty of sandwiches and coffee, they had spent their time watching cable TV with sporadic glances out the window, waiting for Drake to appear.

Beaver had also managed to steal a black van, which they had secured safely in the hotel's garage to avoid detection by the police who regularly patrolled the area.

They had reported the movements of the pair on a daily basis to Johnston, and after Drake had obtained his Egyptian visa from the consulate, thought it was about time to make their move, fearing that Drake might leave the country at any moment. Their plan was to grab the girl and use her as a bargaining chip.

Had it not been for Drake's extraordinary sixth sense, their plan could have succeeded. The snatch attempt on the corner of Whitehall Place had failed, and the bungled chase that followed only served to stoke the anger welling up inside the two pursuers. With both Drake and the girl now holed up in the tower with only one narrow exit, they had one last chance to complete their task.

CHAPTER 8

Geeorge's system was now pumped full of adrenaline. He knew they were in a tight spot with only one way out, which would also lead them right into the hands of their hefty stalkers.

From the entrance turnstile, they crossed over the moat into Byward Tower, the innermost of the three gate towers, then ran down Water Lane.

Turning left, George cut the pace a little as they walked through Bloody Tower while catching their breath. It was here that Sir Walter Raleigh wrote his *History of the World* while a prisoner under the reign of James I.

George decided it was best to look for sanctuary in the armory located in the central White Tower complex in order to avoid being spotted by Beaver, who was now on his way down Water Lane, having left Harman at the exit guzzling a Galaxy chocolate bar. George pulled on Sherry and hastened her toward the great central keep.

Two yeoman wardens looked suspiciously at the young couple as they raced up the makeshift wooden steps leading into the royal armories. The collection of armor and weapons took shape during the reign of Henry VIII who completely restocked the building and also set up his own workshop in Greenwich to make fine armor for himself and his court. In medieval times this tower was lived in by the royal families of the era and represented the seat of government. Now it was a potential refuge.

George peered out through one of the double-slit windows overlooking the main entrance and saw that Beaver had guessed his move. Turning to Sherry, he said, "I think it may be best if we split up for a while, as this guy will be looking for two people on the run. Quickly join the tour group in the next room, and try to keep yourself in the middle to avoid detection."

"What are you going to do?" she murmured as she squeezed George's palm.

"I have to try and lead him away from you. Give me half an hour, then break away from the group, and look for me in the Jewel House. It will be safer there with plenty of guards around."

George didn't like leaving Sherry on her own in what was definitely an alien environment; however, this was the only plan he could come up with. To avoid revealing her, George backtracked to the entrance passing through the Chapel of St. John the Evangelist. He then passed into the tournament room, which was roped off and clear of any visitors. The room was entirely devoted to armor used in war exercises and would be awkward for one person to search. Perching himself behind one of the masterpieces worn by Henry VIII, George held his breath, knowing Beaver was just around the corner.

Beaver dodged the ropes and barged into the room in his usual sturdy style and seeing it was clear, he pulled out his silenced automatic pistol. He laughed and said, "Don't make me waste my time looking for you. I know you're in here, and you know what I want. Give me the parchment, and I'll let you and the girl go unharmed!"

While inching slowly behind the suit of armor, George managed to prize a mace that had been loosely hanging behind the exhibit without making a sound. Beaver continued to bark his presence, and George carefully lined his body like a silhouette.

Beaver saw Drake make his move, raised the pistol, and fired off a round. Fortunately for George, the bullet only creased him slightly on one side, and despite the surprise at getting hit, he managed to pull the mace back over his shoulder and hit Beaver on the back of his neck. Beaver fell to the floor like a sack of potatoes and dropped the gun. Drake stooped down and collected the abandoned revolver and slipped it into his jacket pocket.

So as not to cause a scene, he quietly exited the room and mingled back into the crowd that was milling around in the adjacent room admiring the ancient armor.

George felt his shirt sticking to him and noticed a large red stain extending down his right side. To conceal the wound, he closed his jacket. Outside the White Tower, George headed off in the direction of the Jewel House and stopped off at a public toilet located outside the entrance. Finding an unused cubicle, he took off his jacket and shirt and inspected the wound. Fortunately, the bullet had only grazed him, tearing off a thin slice of flesh and narrowly missing his rib cage.

Had it hit bone, the consequences would have been disastrous.

Not surprisingly, his lesion was still seeping some blood; however, the coagulation process was already taking some effect. George grabbed the toilet roll, tore away the first few sheets (which he considered soiled), then used the rest, turning them into a makeshift swab. He neatly tucked away the pile of tissue under his shirt pressing it against the wound. He then put on his leather jacket, flushed the toilet, and made for the neighboring sink to wash his hands.

As the water poured over his wrists and fingers into the white ceramic bowl, he cringed as he saw the water turn a deep crimson. He always hated the sight of blood ever since the day he had fallen off a fence onto a glass bottle that almost severed his right leg when he was only four.

He walked outside into the fresh air, thinking that Beaver would still be looking for them assuming he had recovered from the blow. George's shoulder throbbed as he pushed the door leading into the Jewel Room. It was a darkened space surrounded with glass cases that housed the most valuable jewel collection in the world. Crowns from the early kings and queens right up to Queen Elizabeth II were displayed in all their finery.

Looking intently at the Star of Africa, emblazoned into the coronation crown, Sherry waited for George to arrive. When she first spotted him staggering down the central corridor, she knew something was wrong and ran toward him. His face was pale, and the grimace of pain written in his expression worried her.

"What's happened?" she inquired putting her arm around him.

"Ouch!" George said. "I've been shot. It's nothing to worry about. The bullet only grazed me, but let me tell you, I don't ever want to get shot again, because if this hurts, it must be hell if you really get hit."

"Please, don't talk this way. We should go to the police and tell them, then let you get properly patched up."

"Definitely not. If we do that, the police will ask us why we were being chased, then ask about the scroll and where it came from, and that would scupper our plans. Let's get out of here and leave the country before they get onto us. If we can make it to the Tower Hill underground station, we can catch an eastbound tube, slip into Victoria, and catch the next train to Paris. We have everything we need and can even post the scroll from there, once the heat is off."

"Hmmm, Paris sounds nice. Let's get going, and remind me at Victoria to get some antiseptic cream and bandages for your wound. And a new shirt would probably be a good idea too," Sherry said.

"Quick, let's get a move on," George said, as he thought he saw Beaver enter the Jewell Room having caught a glimpse of what appeared to be his bulky frame through the glass casing of the queen's coronation crown. Fortunately, the exit was in the other direction, and George took hold of Sherry's wrist and gently eased her through the maze of showcases. He set a medium pace so as not to arouse any suspicion or be noticed by Beaver who almost certainly must have one hell of a headache!

Once outside they made a quicker pace backtracking the way they had originally came. Fortunately, as they reached the entrance, two policemen were on patrol, and all Harman could do was give them a menacing stare and follow them up the hill toward the underground entrance.

George thought Harman might give up, but instead he took out a six-inch switchblade and ran straight for George, who was still a bit woozy from his injury. As he reached him, Harman slashed the razor-sharp blade, severing the straps holding up George's bag. He saw the postal package inside, pulled it out, and ran in the opposite direction. George couldn't believe it.

"Sherry! They got the dammed scroll."

"Never mind, darling. I think it will take Johnston some time to figure out what it's all about since I'm no longer there to interpret for him. I reckon if we leave now, we can get the next piece of the puzzle before he makes his next move."

"Not a bad idea. I think this mystery is really getting to you, Ms. Holmes," George joked. "With the change in circumstances, I think we'd better take the tube to Heathrow and get on the next plane to Cairo. Thank god he dropped the bag, so we at least still have our passports."

It was a long ride to Heathrow and necessitated a change at Piccadilly Circus. As it wasn't rush hour the crowds were light, so at least they could sit.

Once at Heathrow, George found the British Airways ticket counter and got their tickets for the flight that evening. Since they still had several hours to kill, he suggested they get their clothes in order and clean up at one of the nearby airport hotels.

Heathrow, apart from being one of the world's busiest airports, also had a bustling shopping mall. Here, George managed to pick up a small travel bag, additional changes in clothing, as well as necessary medical supplies and toiletries.

Armed with bags in both hands, they exited the terminal and took a short taxi ride to the nearest hotel and booked a room. Once in the room, George removed his jacket and tore off the now stiff bloodstained shirt. It was so clotted that as it came off, laden with caked toilet paper, the rough and newly formed scabs pulled away, reopening the wound. Fortunately, the flow of blood was light, and the best thing to do was get it cleaned and properly bandaged.

Sherry helped George into the shower and gently rubbed him down. In order not to stain the towels or create any suspicion, they used tissues to carefully dry the lesion. Then they covered it with antiseptic cream, and she wrapped some gauze around it, followed by a bandage.

"Wow, what a day. Johnston must have an even darker side to him than I'd previously suspected. Maybe he's involved in some kind of black-market trading, which is another possibly why the antiquities department asked me to keep an eye on him," Sherry said.

"I didn't realize you were a secret sleuth, in addition to being such a fantastic, and might I say, beautiful Egyptologist. I'd like to believe this is a union brought on by fate and that we're somehow destined to be together," George replied, still enjoying her medicinal touch.

"Oh my, the true romantic. I think we'll be in for a very interesting ride, and I look forward to being an integral part of Team Drake! And on that note I'm going to take a quick shower myself."

While Sherry took her shower, George couldn't resist jumping back into the steamy chamber. Grabbing hold of Sherry in a fit of passion, he pulled her close and embraced her. As if the end of the world was fast approaching, he quickly guided her back to the bedroom. Tossing their towels to the ground, they dove under the sheets, desperate to make love and release the pent-up emotions that had been steadily building since their first encounter.

"I wasn't quite expecting that, but I have to say you're quite the stud, Mr. Drake."

"Touché, Sherry! And, likewise, you're quite the vixen. I think we're both in for one hell of a ride, and I certainly couldn't do this without you."

Both now ardently satisfied by their joint fit of eroticism, George ordered some sandwiches and tea, and as a precaution, he telephoned the hotel operator for a wake-up call, just in case they fell asleep.

The food arrived in ten minutes. They ate ravenously, not having had anything in their stomachs since the very quick breakfast prior to all the action that morning. Afterward, Sherry lay down next to George, resting her head on his good shoulder. Relaxed, they both drifted into a deep sleep, thinking about the exciting journey ahead and what possible treasures could be unearthed if they managed to find the next clue ahead of Johnston.

CHAPTER 7

K nowing they were going to get a handsome reward from Johnston, Beaver and Harman jumped into a taxi and headed back to the British Museum.

Harman recounted his catch and how he had cornered them just before they managed to get away, as Beaver nursed his sore head, desperate for a couple of Panadols.

Johnston was pleased with their success, though grumbled at how long it had taken them to get the scroll. He still needed their services knowing full well that Drake was on the loose and probably on his way to Egypt.

Getting up from his old Georgian-style wooden desk, Johnston strode across his office to an old Chubb combination safe. He rotated the central dial backward and forward until the last digit fell in place, then pulled the lever with a slight hint of aggression and opened the door. Inside the safe was a stack of bank notes in various denominations neatly secured in piles with elastic bands. Extracting a stack of Sterling-denominated notes he expertly peeled off 160 crisp fifty-pound notes and quickly closed the door and secured the safe again by flicking the dial.

Beaver had noticed the stack of cash and thought he could raise the stakes again; however, at the last minute, he decided it was better to play along with Johnston and maybe grab the cash from the safe later on as it would be an easy one to crack.

Johnston returned to his desk and beckoned Harman to hand over the scroll, "Come on, you idiot, I haven't got all day. Don't you realize we're in a race against time!?"

Harman wasn't used to this type of verbal abuse and nervously approached the desk. He handed over the parchment and quickly grabbed the stack of notes fearing Johnston might renege on the deal.

"Okay, boys, here's a mobile pager. Keep it switched on all the time. I'll need you to move your ugly asses to Egypt in the next few days, and I want you to be ready. You're now employees of the museum and have a special clearance to join our archeological team in Luxor. At Luxor, a gentleman will meet you by the name of Selim bin Laden. Selim is not a man to be fooled with; he's ten times more ruthless than you and would not hesitate to cut your throats. I've been dealing with him for some time now, as he runs a small smuggling business dealing in Egyptian artefacts. I've already briefed Selim that you'll be keeping an eye on Drake and the girl. If it looks like Drake is going to tip off the local authorities about what they're looking for, get rid of them! Also, if he finds whatever it is that's out there before us, the same rule applies. Now let's get back to business. I need a couple days to get this scroll deciphered. I want you both to keep off the juice and stay clean. When I call you, you can make your way to Heathrow and collect your tickets. I suggest you get a bag ready to leave at a moment's notice."

"Is that all for now?" Beaver said.

"Yes, you can leave now, and don't forget to shut the door on the way out."

Johnston looked over the scroll and wondered what secrets were hidden within the strange illustrations. He would soon work it out and beat Drake to the spoils.

Once they were out on the street, Beaver grabbed Harman by the collar.

"Aren't we forgetting something, asshole?"

"What are you driving at?" Harman screeched.

"Oh, come on. The frigging money, you fool! Let's divide it up."

Harman withdrew the wad of banknotes, and Beaver grabbed for the cash.

"What the hell's wrong with you? We're a team now and have to learn to trust each other," Harman said.

"Okay, matey, although it will probably take some time to adjust to your puny company."

Moving across the road into a small park opposite the museum, Harman found a bench and sat down. He counted out Beaver's share and handed it over.

Beaver, as suspicious as ever, double-checked Harman's counting, then slapped him on the shoulder.

"Not bad for a couple days of work, huh? Let's go celebrate!"

Johnston had locked himself in his office and refused to receive any calls or interruptions. He stared at the scroll and reached for one of his reference books to start the deciphering process. He marveled at the surrounding pictures and knew this was going to lead to something the world had never witnessed, something that would surpass Howard Carter's discovery of Tutankhamun's tomb in the early twenties.

Unfortunately, without the help of Sherifa, the interpretation of the scroll would be far more difficult; however, Johnston was not head of the Egyptian section of the British Museum for nothing. Prior to joining the museum, he had studied Egyptology at Cambridge, where he graduated with honors. He followed this up with a number of years in Egypt excavating new areas at Sakkara, just outside Cairo. From there he moved to the Egyptian Museum in Tahrir Square in Cairo, with the responsibility of assisting in surveying the contents of its basement and cataloging the thousands of exhibits which had never been exhibited.

It was while Johnston was in Egypt that he met up with Selim bin Laden, who was not really Egyptian. He had survived on forged documents and built up a very lucrative business backed by smuggling antiquities and drugs. He was certainly not a religious man; however, he had cleverly conned those around him into thinking he was one of the great Muslim freedom fighters who would help free Egypt from the tight grip of the evil West.

Selim had a luxurious compound in a village outside of Luxor guarded by armed bandits. It was these bandits who were involved in the slaughter of tourists at one of the temples several years back, though nothing could ever be proved, and no one would ever question or insinuate that Selim had been behind this.

Johnston, by using the cover of the British Museum, had made a fortune handling stolen Egyptian antiquities. He had done this by establishing an import-export business in Marseilles. Cotton bales from Egypt would be sent by steamer out of Alexandria, where Selim had a freight forwarding company. Small objects would first be carefully wrapped in gauze, then baled up in cotton. Because the bales were large and the objects in question "drug free," the authorities never caught on. In addition, these shipments were not regular and would only be made three or four times a year making discovery more difficult for customs inspectors, who were already on Selim bin Laden's payroll.

Once Johnston had learned of Drake's scroll, he alerted Selim of the papyrus and said they needed to find the place in advance of the antiquities department so they could raid as much of the uncatalogued find as possible.

CHAPTER 8

Drake woke up to a ringing phone. He picked up the receiver and listened to the drone of the computerized wake-up call. He slammed down the receiver and woke up Sherry.

"Come on, we need to get ready for our flight," he said.

"God, am I tired. It seems like I haven't slept for a week," Sherry said as she made her way to the bathroom.

Once again George found himself excited as he snuck in and cuddled up behind her.

"Maybe we can catch a couple hours on the plane if we're lucky. Flying makes me very sleepy, and I always manage to get some shuteye," George said as Sherry entered the shower. "I've been giving some thought to how we should proceed and think we should avoid Cairo."

"What do you mean?" she shouted from the shower

"Well, Johnston's bound to be looking for us. In addition, as we're going to have to do a bit of diving in Kom Ombo, we'll need to get in some practice as well as procure equipment. I think we should go somewhere like Sharm El-Sheikh first, then take a flight to Luxor."

"That's a great idea. I have friends in Sharm who run a diving center, and at the same time, we can have a couple days of holiday recuperating in the Sinai sun. After several months in England, I'm desperate to get my tan back!"

"That's settled then. As soon as we get to Cairo, we'll change terminals and get the first connection to Sharm that's available."

George decided it was better not to shower, as this could potentially aggravate his wound. Instead he washed his face, dressed up in his new shirt, and went downstairs to settle the bill.

Returning to the room he called out: "All aboard Flight 401 to Cairo!"

Sherry was still blow drying her lush, curly, and slightly unruly raven hair that George had begun to love and needed a few more minutes to get ready.

They had no heavy luggage so there was no need to get to the check-in too early. Nevertheless, George was anxious to get the formalities over and have boarding passes in hand. Only then would he relax and look forward to arriving in Cairo, a destination he had longed to go to since early childhood.

The journey was uneventful and passed relatively quickly. Flying time to Cairo was only four and half hours with a two-hour time differential. By the time they had checked through immigration it was 4:00 a.m. Despite the early hour, the airport was bustling with activity, and hustlers looking for tips bombarded them.

The local terminal was a much older building located almost two kilometers from the new international terminal. A short taxi ride got them there within ten minutes where they established that the next Egypt Air flight to Sharm El-Sheikh was at 6:00 a.m. Sherry, being an Egyptian, purchased the tickets and got a special deal. Unfortunately, George had to suffer the purge of being a foreigner and cough up the full fare. Even though the price differential was not substantial, George complained over the discrimination.

"George, you're going to have to live with this in Egypt. How do you think our country survives?

We have to tax foreigners as much as possible and also subsidize locals who don't have the same earning capacity. The average salary in Egypt is only about two hundred dollars per month."

"I know. I was only giving you a bit of a hard time, and you took the bait."

Passing through into the terminal waiting area, George noticed the building was full of tourists, some in beachwear obviously bound for Sharm El-Sheikh or Hurghada with others heading off to Luxor and Aswan to see the marvels of these two ancient cities.

With the air was full of trepidation, George ordered a coffee to calm himself.

Their flight was full, and after dropping off passengers at Sharm El-Sheikh, they would then proceed to Luxor before returning to Cairo later in the day, ready to do the round trip again. George made a mental note to book them onto the next leg of this flight after they'd had a couple days to rest and procured all the equipment they needed for exploring the tunnel at Kom Ombo.

Flying time was only forty minutes, and from the window they had a marvelous view of the Sinai Peninsula. Sherry recounted some history of the area and how Israel had taken this territory from Egypt in the sixties and how after the Camp David Accords had returned it back to Egypt, although in spite had demolished almost all the buildings. Since then hundreds of hotel developments had sprouted up luring guests to the crystal-clear waters of the Red Sea and the wonders of Ras Mohammed National Park. She was so busy giving the guided tour that she didn't notice the plane touch down on a narrow airstrip adjacent to the coastline.

Sharm El-Sheikh International Airport was a quaint regional airport with only a small terminal building able to serve two flights at any given time. As they had no luggage, they were able to walk straight through and hitch a ride on a curtsey hotel shuttle waiting outside.

Sherry recommended the Movenpick Jolie Ville Resort located on Naama Bay, as this was ideally situated in the heart of the best beach area and near all the main dive centers.

Sitting in the back of the shuttle, they had to wait another ten minutes while other guests collected their bags and got on. The subsequent ride into town only took ten minutes.

The outside air was nice and crisp with a cool westerly breeze blowing in off the pristine azure waters of the Red Sea. The drive along the coast road into town took them past many hotels that occupied every available access point to the water whether beachfront or rocky cliffs. On their right were still more hotels and shops and beyond that a small stretch of desert landscape leading toward the mountains of the famed Sinai Desert and Moses's acquisition of the Ten Commandments.

The hotel consisted of clusters of one-story units that stretched all the way from the lobby area down to the beach. In the lobby, some folk musicians greeted arriving guests with indigenous pipes and drums. A welcome thirst quencher, called *karkadeh*, was also handed to each guest, which was a purple juice made from the hibiscus flower and was very palatable.

As with the air tickets, Egyptian nationals benefited from much better room rates than foreigners, so Sherry took care of the check-in process. Once the formalities were completed, an electric golf cart ferried them to their room, which had a plaque on the door stating the room had once been used by the Israeli prime minister during a peace summit staged at the hotel several years back.

The room was basic—very much geared toward beach-going visitors—and perfect for their requirements.

Sherry picked up the phone and asked the operator to connect her with an old family friend named Mohamed "Sunny" Talal. Sunny was one of the real entrepreneurs of Sharm El-Sheikh having lived there all his life. He owned several hotels and diving centers and would be an ideal source for the equipment they needed.

"Sunny, is that you? I've just got back to Egypt from London and thought a few days of R and R in Sharm would do me good. I've also come with a close friend, a Britisher, but don't worry, he's really nice. We're actually very keen to practice some diving and would like to get some night diving experience if possible?"

Sunny boomed out a traditional Egyptian welcome. He then said, "Hell! I'd better keep on talking. I know what you hamza's are like: once you're on the phone, you can hardly get a word in! Don't worry, I'm only joking, but seriously, it's really good to hear you're in town, and whatever you need, just remember that my house is your house. As far as equipment, you can take what you need. Why spend your hard-earned cash when I have a dive shop with plenty of gear in storage? I suggest when you're both fully rested, we meet down at Red

Sea Divers, which is within walking distance from your hotel."

"Sounds good," Sherry replied as she beamed a smile at George and threw a thumbs-up.

"Shall we say five this afternoon? After we've checked out the basic equipment and scheduled you in with some practice diving, we can stop by a bar and grab a couple beers. To reach my shop just head toward the sea, and as soon as you hit the little boulevard in front of the hotel beach, fork right, and we're about five hundred yards on the right-hand side. And if you miss the sign, it's opposite a small fish restaurant called The Spotted Grouper."

"Wow! I think the hospitality life suits you! You really do know how to look after people well. We'll have to make sure we come here more often and get thoroughly spoiled. We'll see you then! I'm looking forward to catching up with you."

With formalities taken care of, Sherry dived onto the bed next to George and gave him a quick bear hug.

"Be careful, darling!" George moaned with a grimace. "Don't forget my side is still pretty sore from the tower escapade. Now, tell me, what did Sunny say?"

Sherry recounted her phone call and the planned rendezvous at Sunny's dive center.

"As you rightly said, it sounds fantastic. Not only can we get kitted up, we'll also be able to organize a night dive, preferably with some confined space maneuvers? Don't let's forget, when we get to Kom Ombo, we won't know what that murky pool will reveal, if anything."

"Oh, you can be such a pessimist. I have a good feeling about this, and while I like Sharm, I'd much prefer to be on my way to Upper Egypt as soon as possible."

"Okay, okay, point taken. Now, rather than moping around here, let's get down to the beach and enjoy a few rays and have a taste of the Red Sea!" George suggested as he playfully slapped Sherry's buttocks.

Sherry quickly put away their possessions and suggested they stop at one of the hotel boutiques to pick up some swimwear.

"I guess the authorities here are not too keen on skinny dipping," George joked as they walked out into the blazing sunshine.

The shops were located in a small arcade adjacent to the hotel swimming pool easily visible by the excess quantity of souvenirs stacked haphazardly in front of the already crammed stores. Grabbing anything that looked the part; they squeezed into the tiny changing cubicle to check out their wares. George emerged first, and apart from the still-rosy gash on his back looked a suitable candidate for Muscle Beach. Sherry was not to be outclassed and donned a *Baywatch*-style red one piece, which sensuously revealed all the contours of her petite body.

They told the shop assistant that they were heading straight for the beach so there was no need to bag the goods, which included two pairs of flip-flops and a beach bag to store their earlier attire. In addition, they added some SPF-8 protective oil to cut down on the UV intake and some light reading material. George paid the man after a fruitless attempt at bartering with his credit card. Fortunately, Sherry was on hand to throw an Egyptian insult before the final price was amicably agreed upon.

Thankfully, the hotel was not too busy, so it was easy to find a good spot on the beach at the shoreline. Towels were provided on entry in exchange for towel cards that had been given to them while checking in. All eyes focused on them, and a few snide remarks or rude jokes passed between the attendants on duty, which Sherry swiftly put an end to with another sharp interjection in Arabic. Slightly shocked by the repost, the uniformed attendants sprang to attention and couldn't do enough to make the rest of their stay on the beach as comfortable as possible. George was really impressed and reveled over all the fussing.

George settled down, having applied copious amounts of the sunscreen to his torso, and immersed himself in a Clive Cussler novel and the marvels of Dirk Pitt and NUMA, the organization he worked for. His wound had neatly closed, and it was nice to be finally free of the dressing that he had tossed in the trash after changing into his swimsuit.

The sea was crystal clear, and even using the most basic mask and snorkel was enough to see a remarkable array of marine life. About fifty yards offshore coral reefs were scattered about providing habitats for many species of tropical fish. The majestic emperor angelfish was aggressively guarding his territory like an angry general. Even the cute little clownfish with their striking orange and white stripes defiantly patrolled their homes darting in and out of the protective arms of sea anemones immune to the stinging tentacles. George enjoyed a brief cat-and-mouse chase with these feisty little creatures by invading their space and reaching out for the anemones. Fearlessly and oblivious to the size differential, time and time again, the tiny clownfish made a rush for George's finger before quickly returning to the safety of the anemones' protective custody. Brightly colored parrotfish and surgeonfish rushed to and frow making the occasional pit stop to chomp away at tasty lumps of coral. At the bottom, which was only about ten meters down, beautiful but dangerous lionfish puffed out their fins and glided gracefully, often turning in somersaults as they looked around with their large, beady eyes for a suitable prey.

It was like another world, and both George and Sherry were very soon free of all the tension that had plagued them over the previous twenty-four hours.

Both their bodies tanned almost immediately. When they returned to their room in the early afternoon to prepare for the meeting with Sunny, their skin tingled as the new color set in.

"Sorry, George, no time for hanky-panky now! We've got to get moving if we're going to make our appointment with Sunny."

"I know," agreed George, "it's just that you look so ravishing in that swimsuit, I even thought of pretending to drown to get you to give me the kiss of life. You really had the *Baywatch* babe look out there."

Having both showered and changed, they headed back to the promenade adjacent to the beach. It was already beginning to fill with tourists, and little shops and street vendors were out in force. There was also a vast numbers of dive shops and tour operators offering dive trips all over the Red Sea.

Sunny's Red Sea Divers was easy to find. In the front was a small shop selling all types of diving equipment and beach merchandise. He had the agency for both US Divers and Technisub, as well as agencies for many other brands of accessories and swimwear. In the rear was a small lecture room and a warehouse full of equipment used by day-rental customers. Sunny had a staff of five that included two full-time instructors who ran courses affiliated with the PADI system.

Both George and Sherry were already accomplished divers with George attaining the rank of a second-class diver under the old BSAC certification. George had done all his training while he lived in Cambridge and had undergone all his practical dives off the British Coast. Sherry, on the other hand, had been diving in the Red Sea since the tender age of ten and was the youngest ever Egyptian to don an underwater breathing apparatus. While she had no official certification, her experience far outweighed that of her English partner in crime!

Sunny was busy in a small workshop at the far end of the warehouse charging up bottles for the next day's dive schedule. A row of ten tanks, all submersed in barrels of cold water to keep them from overheating during the compression process, were lined up against the wall and connected to high-pressure pipes that ultimately fed into a large Bristol compressor located in an adjacent room. The air-intake pipe stretched up through the roof in an attempt to draw in the cleanest possible air devoid of any low-level pollutants.

George hadn't realized what a powerful man Sunny was. He was over six foot tall and nearly as broad. His muscles rippled through his sweat-laden T-shirt ironically depicting a shark taking a bite out of a tourist along with the logo of his Red Sea Divers organization.

"Sherifa, wow, it's good to see you. How long did you say it's been? Too long, for sure." Then, swinging around to George, he added, "And you must be the

English gentleman I heard about!" He gave George a powerful slap on the shoulder

"Well, obviously from your welcome, Sherry didn't tell you everything. I actually caught a piece of lead a couple days back just below where you whacked me," George said.

"Oh, I'm so sorry!" Turning back to Sherry, Sunny said, "If this means what I think it does, are you guys in some form of trouble?"

"Look, it's a long story, and since you suggested having a few beers afterward, I'll tell you everything then. In the meantime, what equipment can we borrow that's reasonably compact? We plan to take a short trip from here and don't want to be too saddled with extra weight and unnecessary items," Sherry said.

Sunny, who was now clearly brimming with intrigue, put his mind on the task at hand and assembled a suitable shopping list.

"Okay, one dive bag between the two of you, I assume, is all you want. In it I'll add two neoprene 'shorty' wet suits, weight belts, and SCUBAPRO regulators with combined pressure and depth gauges. You'll also need the usual masks, fins, and snorkels. As far as tanks are concerned, the smallest I have are single US Divers aluminum Luxfors, which will give you about two thousand psi and approximately forty-minute bottom time at twenty meters. I'll also add a couple pairs of gloves, knives, and lightweight halogen torches. Will this suffice?"

George realized he had been a bit harsh with his initial abrupt welcome and quickly voiced his appreciation. "Sunny, I didn't mean to jump down your throat earlier. This is really too generous of you, and I don't know what to say."

"Come off it, George, this is nothing. I'll have my staff pack up the dive bag and prepare the bottles for you. They'll also arrange to refill them whenever you want. I suggest tomorrow morning you take an easy shore dive, and afterwards, I'll take you to one of the more interesting sights on my boat."

George, now totally taken aback by the massive Egyptian's extreme hospitality, decided to open up more about what they had in mind in terms of preparatory work. "On the subject of diving practice, we're planning to do a spot of cave diving and would really appreciate if you could take us somewhere where we can simulate finning through confined spaces in the dark."

Sunny pondered the request and said, "We don't have any real caves nearby; however, there are dozens of wrecks around. I can take you out to the *Thistlegorm.*"

It's one of our most popular sites, and as you can imagine it has a lot of nooks and crannies. If we go in the afternoon, all the tourist dives will have departed by the time we get there, giving us complete freedom. Also, with the sun going down, you'll get to experience night diving at its best."

Having agreed to the agenda, they all exited and headed for the Movenpick Beach Bar. Sunny ordered three bottles of chilled Sakara beer and launched into a lecture about the improvement in Egyptian brewing and how poor the quality of ale had been until recently.

"I think you'll love this beer. It can match anything coming out of Europe and certainly beats the Americans hands down. Tell me, what do you think?"

"Hmmmm! Excellent! And after what we've been through the last few days, I can't tell you how welcoming this is. Nectar from the gods and possibly the best I've ever had!" George responded with even greater admiration for Sunny and decided to take him into their full confidence about the whole affair by briefing him about the bizarre episode at the

Tower of London, although he didn't go into too much detail about the scroll.

On the other side of the bar an Egyptian man with a hooked nose listened intently to the ongoing conversation. Abu Hussein was an off-duty policeman and bin Laden snitch. Under instructions from bin Laden, he was to monitor their every move and await further instructions. This work paid far better than his daily routine with the local tourist police and also allowed him to sink a few beers in order to look less conspicuous.

Over the course of the next two hours, Abu learned that Sunny was going to take the two foreigners out on his boat the following afternoon to the *Thistlegorm* wreck. From what he knew about wrecks in the Red Sea, this was well marked and located a few miles to the northeast of a place known as Shag Rock on the southern tip of Sha'ab Ali in the Gulf of Suez. They were to meet at his boat moored at Sharm Harbor at 4:30 p.m. a few miles from the hotel. It appeared they were aiming to try and reach the wreck site just before dark and were going to practice a night dive on the wreck. Abu wondered why on earth they were attempting a night dive so far away and decided it was time to make a discrete exit and report his findings. Sunny's boat was well known so it would be easy to pick up the trail.

Settling his account, Abu walked off with a Cheshire-like smile and pondered what bin Laden had in store for them.

The remainder of the evening passed uneventfully, and George and Sherry decided to call it a day. Signing off the tab to the room, George arranged to pick up the gear from Red Sea Divers in the morning so they could at least get a little training in by way of a beach dive. It was unlikely their depth would exceed ten meters, so if they logged the time and depth properly, they would avoid having to make any decompression stops on the *Thistlegorm* dive later in the day.

Back in their room, George congratulated Sherry on her excellent organization. Having Sunny as an ally would be very useful.

"The only matter I'm a little concerned about is why we have to go so far to do a spot of night diving. I just didn't have the heart to say no after all he's done for us."

"I know exactly what you mean; however, this is typical Egyptian hospitality. He knows we're shooting off elsewhere and is keen to show us a good time. I'm sure the wreck is probably the best dive within relatively easy reach from here." Sherry let out a drawn-out, whispery yawn. "Wow am I whacked! Lights out!"

CHAPTER 9

Unfortunately for Drake, Johnston was not a man to allow anyone to get in his way. He assumed that Drake and Sherifa must have already left the country and were either on their way or had arrived in Egypt. The question bugging him was what their next move was going to be and how he could possibly head them off and intercept whatever it was they were after.

Although Johnston now had the original scroll, he still hadn't figured out the interpretation of the detailed hieroglyphics contained on it, and every time he looked at it, his frustration seethed into a boiling rage enhanced by high blood pressure caused from an unhealthy balance of red meat, alcohol, and lack of exercise. He still continued to gently caress the ancient papyrus and drool over the minuscule drawings, desperate to seek the answer to his dreams of being the next Howard Carter.

Johnston's phone rang. Mustapha El Din, his opposite at the Ministry of Antiquities, had some news for him that drew a sweeping evil smirk across his face. El Din had, through his connections in the tourist police, managed to establish the whereabouts of Drake and the girl. According to the equally overweight El Din, they were holed up at the Hotel Movenpick Jolie Ville located at the Red Sea resort of Sharm El-Sheikh.

Johnston was so pleased with El Din's work, and his mind raced ahead to figure out what he must now do to solve his dilemma. He concluded that this would be money well spent.

After putting down the receiver for a short while, he flicked through his telephone directory and extracted Beaver's pager contact and after dialing him, waited impatiently for the call back.

"Right, you two," he barked. "I want you both on the next flight to Cairo. I've arranged for Selim bin Laden to meet you at Cairo International Airport. He will then drive you to Sharm El-Sheikh where you will find our two birds nesting in the Movenpick Hotel. Do whatever you think is necessary to keep them out of our way, just don't kill them yet. Your tickets will be ready for you at the BA counter at Heathrow. You don't have much time, so grab whatever you need and get moving! And make sure you don't miss the flight, or there'll be hell to play!"

Johnston hung up and sat back in his old weather-beaten Chesterfield sofa. The musty relic from one of London's finest old gentlemen's clubs was an addition to his office that he often used to ponder unanswered questions, in this case the Drake scroll, which lay on the seat next to him along with a scribble pad of notes. Beads of sweat dripped from his brow as he felt himself get back into the race again and pitch slightly ahead of his adversaries who he knew must have the answer to the puzzle. This infuriated him further, although he remained confident that he would soon decipher the code. He also knew that he would probably have to try and keep them both alive until the next clue was solved. The thought of Drake getting to the spoils first sent an irritating shiver down his spine.

Beaver and Harman decided it was better to travel light and just grab an overnight bag along with their newly acquired museum travel documents, rather than risk missing the flight and incurring the wrath of Johnston.

On arrival at Cairo International Airport, one of Selim bin Laden's henchmen met the pair as they walked into the arrivals area and shuffled them through to a small, drab office where their travel documents could be checked and stamped in private. The policeman manning this office was also on Selim's extensive payroll, and any criminal record the goons might have had would be conveniently disregarded and entry into the country simplified.

"That was certainly well organized," Harman said as they waited for the cop to finish.

"Cor blimey, mate! I don't think I could take standing in those long lines outside. I haven't got the patience and would almost certainly pick a fight with anyone trying to jump the queue, which seems to be a national past time here," Beaver replied.

The disheveled policeman handed back their passports and with a throaty growl welcomed the two visitors to Egypt.

With the formalities concluded, they were hurriedly passed on to another bin Laden associate who took them through the last leg of the well-worn terminal, past the baggage-claim area, yet another set of officials, and finally into the arrivals hall. As they eased their way through the last set of doors, they were greeted by a blast of warm air and an unusual mass of sweaty bodies congregating at the exit waiting for inbound friends and relatives.

Both men had obtuse bloodshot eyes and hefty hangovers from too much booze on the near five-hour flight, and their body temperaments were almost at a flash point.

Selim bin Laden had arranged transport, as promised. Outside the terminal building, among a swarm of blue-and-white airport taxis, was a portly Egyptian clad in a multicolored *galabia*, which had more of a resemblance of a Victorian nightgown but was actually considered by many as the national dress. The man who introduced himself as Ahmed gestured them to follow him through the dusty parking lot where he had an old Peugeot 504 Estate car waiting.

Harman grinned at Beaver who knew exactly what was on his mind. By the look of the car, they both wondered how on earth Ahmed had gotten to the airport, let alone was going to ferry them a few hundred miles to Sharm El-Sheikh. The rusty bucket was well weathered and appeared held together by body-repair puddy. It had an enormous number of scrapes, dents, and greasy fingerprints.

"My, oh my! How far is this baby going to get us?" Harman remarked.

Beaver ignored the statement, more anxious to learn about their final destination and what Johnston had concocted with Selim bin. As he climbed into the back seat of the Peugeot, he shook Ahmed's hand and decided to make friendly conversation.

"Ahmed, my dear friend, thanks for meeting us. I understand we're to be taken to a place on the Red Sea called Sharm El-Sheikh. Will Selim bin Laden meet us there?"

"So sorry, mister, I'm afraid my English is not very good. All I know is that I'm to collect you from the airport and take you to a villa in Sharm where you will be given further instructions. I suggest you rest, as the drive will take us four or five hours."

Beaver turned to Harman who had just finished disposing a booger from his nose.

"Oh Christ, I wish you'd stop quarrying into your nostrils all the time; it's a disgusting habit. How many times have I told you to clean up your act? Look, we better try and grab some shut-eye while this geezer drives, as I suspect we're going to have a long day tomorrow."

"Get off my case," Harman whined. "You keep to your side of the car, and I'll keep to mine. Wake me when we get there."

Both men collapsed into a deep sleep as Ahmed drove them across the Sinai Peninsula.

In Sharm El-Sheikh, they were finally deposited at a small apartment complex in Naama Bay, fairly close to their prey who were currently being watched twenty-four-seven by one of bin Laden's stooges.

A man by the name of Jassim, who was also a bin Laden lieutenant, occupied the apartment. He sported a black patch over one eye, and from the look of his face had suffered colossal burns, as the skin was blotchy and scarred. Jassim apologized for his appearance and recounted how he had been a tank commander during the Six-Day War. His tank had taken a direct hit from an Israeli bomber. The tank exploded in flames, and he was fortunate enough to have been thrown clear of his turret, although most of his body had been severely burned.

After he had emerged from hospital, Jassim was unable to find fitting employment, until Selim came across him at a military-veteran hangout in the Pyramid Road district in Giza. Selim was beefing up his private force and knew that Jassim would make an excellent leader who asked few questions relative to the tasks at hand.

Jassim had been with Selim for five years and had built up a ruthless band of terrorists operational from a hacienda-type stronghold in Upper Egypt. They had been responsible for countless murders including those of some tourists in Luxor and Cairo. Jassim showed no remorse for his part in it and explained that they were fighting a war against the country's presidential system, which they considered to be a puppet of the American government. Finance for the operation was provided through a slush fund gifted by the Iraqis who encouraged bin Laden to destabilize the country.

Johnston had become involved by accident and through his own greed. It was after a visit to Luxor three years back, when he discovered he could easily smuggle out priceless antiquities and auction them off to private collectors. The funds were split with bin Laden who began to amass a vast fortune and as a result became untouchable. Interpol was aware of the organization's structure but had been unable to apprehend any of its leaders. Bin Laden rarely left his hacienda preferring to command his activities from a state-of-the-art control center located in a bunker deep inside his ranch complex. The bunker had been converted from an ancient-Nubian tomb and required virtually no additional tunnelling. It was because of this, its existence was virtually unknown except for a few key personnel, Jassim included.

If everything went according to plan, Beaver and Harman would probably never come face-to-face with the reclusive bin Laden. From what they had ascertained about this ruthless individual in the short time since their arrival they were keen to get the job completed and leave as quickly as possible with minimum fuss.

Jassim explained that Drake and Sherifa had arrived early that morning and had spent most of the time at their hotel, although that evening they had met with a local businessman at a dive center. Abu, one of Jassim's observers had reported in after having tailed the two to the hotel beach bar, where he learned of their forthcoming expedition to the *Thistlegorm* wreck.

"What do you think we should do?" asked Jassim.

Beaver took the initiative and fired off a series of questions and instructions in order to regain the upper hand. Harman realized he was out of his depth and decided to sit down and listen to the two thrash out their next course of action.

"Have you got a fast boat we can use? I'll also need two sets of diving equipment, two dive scooters, some C-4 with underwater detonators, and additional small weapons. A trip to the local abattoir could also be useful as I think we can put an end to this façade tomorrow evening!"

Harman, on hearing the shopping list, perked up and registered his total confusion over what Beaver was concocting, which was also totally out of line with the instructions that they had received from Johnston.

"Look, you driveling idiot, diving accidents are commonplace, and all we're going to do is stimulate a situation where our friends are going to experience one and disappear."

"How so?" Harman asked.

"We'll get to the wreck site before they do and plant some explosives. We'll use the blood and guts from the abattoir to lure in some sharks to finish them off."

Jassim already had a cigarette boat equipped with a 250HP Evinrude Outboard, a silent runner capable of speeds in excess of forty knots. The boat was frequently used to run contraband for the bin Laden enterprise and had to be capable of outrunning the Egyptian coast guard. The ordnance and diving equipment would be requisitioned from bin Laden and obtained from a small cache hidden away in a warehouse near Dahab about seventy kilometers away.

Bin Laden's cigarette boat was far bigger than Beaver had expected. It had a mono v-hull and a large single cabin area that was normally stuffed with cigarettes or illicit drugs loaded from ships en route from the Far East. The vessel was painted a dull black and no longer had any reflective metal fittings as a countermeasure against detection at night.

Harman looked worried as they made their way up a narrow jetty in Sharm El-Sheikh's old harbor, squeezing their way past swarms of divers who were now disembarking from lines of dive boats parked nose to tail grabbing every inch of possible space along the key.

"What's up with you?" barked Beaver.

"Look, you may be a man of the world, but I'm a bit of a landlubber, and I'm not sure how my sea legs are!" he replied in a cockney drawl.

"No need to worry. Once we put the foot down, you won't notice anyfing," Beaver retorted with a slight chuckle and sarcastic East Ender accent.

Jassim, who had already gone ahead and mustered up the boat and crew, hollered to a Toyota pickup waiting at the other end of the jetty.

"Yallah!" he cried.

The message must have got through as the bodies slouching at the rear end of the pickup suddenly jumped up to attention and started unloading its cargo consisting of two heavy dive bags, one sealed drum, and a couple battered-looking army-surplus steel cylinders.

Beaver, having made a quick mental note of what they were carrying, jumped aboard and rushed over to Jassim. "Hey, I thought we'd agreed that you were going to provide us with a couple underwater scooters."

"Don't worry, my friend, they're already on board, tucked away inside the cabin."

"Good man. I want to be in and out as quickly as possible! Cor blimey! What on earth's that smell?"

"The seal on our drum must be bad," Jassim said. "That's our chum recipe. Let's all get aboard as quickly as possible so we don't draw too much attention."

With a few more "yallahs," a bit of shouting, and a number of prods, the supplies were finally dumped into the cabin, and even as the last porter was climbing back onto the jetty, Jassim was already busy at the bow untying the line connecting them to their berth. Beaver fired the engine into action, although hardly realized it had started due to the extra sound-proofing under the engine housing.

"Your partner in crime better get on board, or we'll leave without him," Jassim said pointing at Harman, who was still milling about on the jetty.

"For Christ's sake, Harman! Get on board this instant!" Beaver insisted.

Harman, whose face had turned from a pale white to a greenish hue, gagged, as he retched bile into his mouth, then quickly reswallowed the putrid material into his already turbulent stomach. This maneuver worked okay once; however, with the next gag, he was unable to hold out as it erupted into a cough, and he puked over the side leaving a slimy trail of partially digested lunch on the surface of Sharm El-Sheikh's murky harbor water.

"Wimp," said Beaver, amused at the weak behavior of his associate.

"Get off my back," Harman whined, feeling a little sorry for himself.

"Okay, mate. Sit yourself down forward, and take in some deep breaths. You'll soon feel a lot better," Beaver said with a little more sympathy.

Jassim pointed the boat out to sea and eased the throttle forward. With each gentle push, the boat surged faster and faster until it was riding tall on the waves leaving a trailing wake that stretched for over half a mile.

As Jassim set the course (27.49' 03"N 33.51 14"E) northeast of Shag Rock, off Sha'ab Ali, and southwest of Ras Muhammed, Beaver made his way into the cabin and started work on preparing the C-4 with remote-controlled detonators specially designed for underwater demolition. Beaver was completely at home and handled the C-4 as if it was Play-Doh in a child's hands. Having armed two packs of C-4, he then checked the remote control to see whether it was properly charged and in working order. A red light flicked on as he set the switch as if ready to detonate. Satisfied, he put the control back into safe mode and moved on to check the rest of the contents of the two dive bags.

CHAPTER 10

Their morning beach dive had gone smoothly, and both were careful not to dive too deep and ensure the time was kept to forty minutes, which was more than enough to get used to their equipment. Having both had plenty of experience in the past, George and Sherry quickly settled down and by the end of the dive had adjusted their breathing techniques to consume minimal air. After lunch, they grabbed their kit, which had been washed down with fresh water, and repacked by the dive center, then made for the harbor.

The harbor was crawling with dive boats and hundreds of divers who were returning from morning excursions. Sunny's boat was a forty-five-foot, three-berth cabin cruiser built by a rather obscure outfit in the United Arab Emirates. While the manufacturer may have been less known than some of its European or American counterparts, the boat had magnificent lines and all the accompanying luxuries.

Sunny spotted them from his "crow's nest" high up on the flybridge and hollered them over using an antique brass megaphone.

"You're in good time. Come on over, and I'll get the engines warmed up so we can cast off and get to our destination a little earlier!"

As the two guests climbed up the narrow gangplank, which was attached to the rear of the boat by a pulley system, the two twin MerCruiser 250HP inboard engines roared to life.

"George, dump your kit in the salon, then untie the rope on the aft deck. Once that's done, climb up here and enjoy the view," Sunny called out.

"Aye, aye, captain!" George retorted putting on his best Long John Silver accent as Sherry made her way to the flybridge.

George arrived a few minutes later and noticed an array of coolers lined up on the sun-bleached teak deck which contained freshly prepared sandwiches and ice-cold Sakara beers.

Sunny looked at George eying the containers. "I know you're thirsty, but I suggest we leave the bulk of the beers for the return leg as we don't want to be pissed on the dive, especially when it's getting dark! Grab a bottle of our local Siwa mineral water to replenish your fluids, and help yourselves to any food if you're hungry."

George followed his advice, and as they pulled out of the harbor he asked about the history of the *Thistlegorm* and what they were likely to see down in the deep-blue yonder.

Sunny enjoyed his leadership role and lecturing on regional dive sites, something he had been doing for over ten years since starting up his Red Sea Divers operation, when he had to do everything from running PADI dive courses to escorting groups of tourists on excursions. Over the years he had also contributed a wealth of data and photographs for hundreds of publications on the Red Sea and its treasure trove of wrecks and diverse wildlife.

Sunny set the coordinates on his autopilot and motioned his two students to sit comfortably and listen to what he was about to say.

"The reason I thought this would be a good dive is it's not particularly deep, and the visibility is usually superb, particularly in the early evening as the sea calms down as if getting ready for bed.

The *Thistlegorm* was an armed British freighter that was bombed by the Germans in 1941 while it was waiting in line to pass through the Suez Canal. The Joseph Thompson Shipyard built it in Sunderland at the end of 1940 for the transport of war materials, and as you can see, she didn't last long. It wasn't until 1956 that the old girl was found again by Jacques Cousteau who, because of the unspoiled beauty of the Red Sea, spent many years surveying the region from aboard *Calypso*, his famous wooden-hulled minesweeper cum survey vessel. I think Cousteau was actually using his dive saucer at the time of this discovery."

"Had she delivered her cargo, or is there still plenty to see?" Sherry asked.

"Good question. The vessel was part of what became known as Operation Crusade, which was a massive allied offensive to reequip Field Marshal Montgomerie's Eighth Army in their battle against Rommel. As the Suez Canal had been closed earlier, she had actually had to circumnavigate Africa and, believe it or not, was only a few miles from her final point of discharge when she was hit. So, to answer your question, she had a full cargo on board that consisted of ammunition, weapons, vehicles, motorcycles, and all sorts of other items needed to keep an army in action. A lot of the superstructure got damaged in the bombing, as some of the munitions aboard also exploded; however, I think you'll be impressed with what you see."

"What else should we be aware of when we're down there? Is there any marine life we should worry about, particularly the hungry ones?" George probed.

"Well, now that you mention it, we will be just in time for dinner. Dusk is the prime feeding time for sharks, although I doubt we'll see any, as they tend to be out hunting in deeper waters. We may be lucky enough to catch a glimpse of a moray eel, as we sometimes see giant morays or smaller honeycomb morays, which are really stunning. However, a word of caution: what we really need to look out for is the sediment and to be careful not to disturb it too much when we're finning inside the wreck, as this can disorient you and make it very easy to get lost! By the way, we won't have time to explore the whole wreck, as there's far too much to see. What I'll do is take you over the main deck, which is only at a depth of about twelve meters, where you can have a look at a couple old rail carriages. There are also two large torpedoes resting there. After this we can fin over to the midsection, where the ship broke into two, then quickly dive down to the bottom where you'll get to see a few tanks that spilled out of the holds. We can also have a quick peak inside one of the holds at the midpoint before returning to the flybridge to savor a few of those chilled beers."

As the ride out was going to take them a couple hours, George decided to take a look around the boat, then check that their equipment was in order, leaving Sherry on the flybridge with Sunny.

While descending the stairwell into the main salon, George noticed what he thought was a wake in the distance reflecting moonlight, most likely churned up by another boat; however, what was more interesting about this particular spark was the speed at which the vessel must have been traveling. Someone was obviously in a hurry to get somewhere. Not thinking any more about it, his mind quickly switched to concentrating on the chore at hand and preparations for the dive ahead.

CHAPTER 11

"We just overtook our friends, who are making about ten knots," Jassim screamed against the wind down to Beaver. "I reckon you'll have a good hour to complete the job!"

"Good," Beaver said, then he banged on the forward cabin window. "Harman, get your fat ass over here. It's time to get suited up so when we reach the wreck's marker buoy, we can just slip over the side, scoot down, lay our charges, and get the hell out of there!"

Sunny was sitting at the controls on his flybridge enjoying the look of a Greek tycoon. "Come up here, and take a refreshment from the icebox," he suggested. "I don't want you guys to dehydrate, even though the sun's on the way down."

"Sounds like a good idea! Are you coming, Sherry?" Drake asked.

Drake scrambled up the stairwell and grabbed a Diet Pepsi from the cooler at Sunny's feet. Sherry was right behind and nuzzled next to Drake, stealing the frosted bottle from his grip and trickled the cool liquid through her tender lips as if tempting Drake. Finishing the bottle, She wiped her mouth with a brush of her bronzed forearm and thanked Drake for the refreshment.

"Well, I never did like the diet version," George said while reaching for a Coke. "I must say, I'm really looking forward to completing the dive and sucking down a few of these ice-cold Sakaras. That's what I'd really kill for; however, we can't really drink and dive," he joked.

"Before we get to the wreck site, and forgive me if I repeat myself, but I think I'd better give you the full rundown and brief you about what to expect," Sunny said. "The wreck is widely acknowledged to be the world's foremost diving attraction and had remained fairly reclusive up to the early nineties. Believe it or not, the wreck was first discovered by a young Jacques Cousteau, who made a short film and documented it; however, afterwards, he gave everyone the slip and deliberately registered the wrong coordinates because he wanted to preserve the site as much as possible. I guess he was probably right as, unfortunately, since its rediscovery and transition into a tourist site, it has begun to deteriorate pretty quickly."

Sherry and George were engrossed, so Sunny continued on.

"She was built by Joseph Thompson and Sons of Sunderland and launched in 1940. The 'Thistle' trademark emanated from her operator, the Albyn Shipping Line, who had a number of other vessels, all carrying a thistle prefix. In May 1941, she was loaded up with supplies for the Eighth Army and relief of Tobruk, as well as two sets of rolling stock for the Egyptian Railways Company. Unfortunately, as the Mediterranean was pretty well under German control, she sailed round the Cape of Good Hope and eventually to Suez, where she anchored in what was thought to be a safe place. As you can expect, this wasn't the case. Two German Heinkel bombers were dispatched from Cyprus to intercept what was perceived to be a large vessel, and one of them managed to discharge its payload on top of her ripping out the bridge and one of the holds and also catapulting the deck cargo into the sea. It sank very quickly with the loss of thirteen lives.

"When we get down there, you'll see she's sitting upright with all her holds exposed, some of which carry interesting cargo consisting of armored vehicles, motorcycles, small arms, ammunition, shells, and so on. It has often been described as a submerged army-surplus store, which in effect it was. The midsection is where the bombs took their toll. As you want to practice in confined spaces, I'll take you down into the number-two hold where you can explore some of the lorries and trailers. We'll pass by a couple railway tenders, which are still on deck, and if we have time we can nip down and see the engine of the seabed."

"Sounds great, Sunny! I can't wait to get down there!" Drake added.

The sun tapered at the edge of the horizon, leaving a beautiful orange glow, which merged upward into a dark-blue sky that, with every passing minute, became purple and eventually left a starlit black sky devoid of any moon.

Using his GPS, it was easy to chart the right course, and as they neared the wreckage site, they saw the marker buoy in the distance and pulled alongside it and tied up to the buoy, since there was no one else around. This way they could jump straight in and use the buoy's anchor chain as a diving aid and easy point of reference. Sunny had a supply of phosphorescent markers to make it easy to spot in the dark and planned to tie some on to the chain once they were down.

"Okay, guys, let's get kitted up and do our buddy checks. As there are three of us, I'll take the lead, and you two stay close behind."

The warmth of the five-mm neoprene wet suits soon engulfed their bodies as they strapped on their weight belts and knives. For this dive, Sunny had brought the latest diving jackets that held the cylinders in place and also acted as buoyancy compensators. Each was also fitted with an octopus second-stage unit, meaning that if any one of them had a problem with their air supply, they could breathe through the octopus and share air from one of the other cylinders without any interference. Powerful flashlights were also in hand to make the viewing experience more pleasurable.

"Before you wet your masks, I suggest you use some of this antifog liquid I found in the US. It's better than spit, and believe me you don't want your mask to fog up on a night dive."

"I must say, now that we're here and about to plunge into the black unknown, I feel a little apprehensive," Sherry whispered to George.

"I heard that," Sunny said. "Once we swim down the anchor line, and you see the wreck coming toward you, you'll forget everything, and I bet you'll even lose track of time, as it's such a wondrous sight."

"Thanks for the reassurance, I needed that. It's like a shot of adrenalin," Sherry said.

"Remember, we're here to have fun, so don't swim too fast, breathe slowly to conserve your air, and above all, avoid hyperventilation. If anyone reaches this point, we'll abort and go back to the beer tent. Now that we're ready, let's carry our jackets and fins to the rear diving platform and do our final checks," Sunny said wrapping up the predive brief.

George decided to act the gentleman and grabbed Sherry's tank cum buoyancy compensator before she could reach it. With his other hand he reached for his own jacket and grimaced with the combined weight.

"Hey girl, you'd better pick up my mask and fins; I can't manage everything," George said.

"And I thought you were superhuman," Sherry said with a playful wink.

Sunny climbed down a wooden ladder to the dive platform located at the stern above the propellers. George, on reaching the ladder, handed down the tanks and remaining gear. Once everything was assembled Sherry climbed down with George bringing up the rear. Mulling over the unknown that lay ahead, they opened the valves on their tanks, strapped on the jackets, and buckled them up ensuring they weren't restricting movement. Sherry purged her second stage blasting out a waft of compressed air and double-checking that it was functioning correctly.

Each diver took one of the flashlights that Sunny had brought along, and as a precaution Sunny added a harpoon gun to his load. He then held up his right hand and with his thumb and forefinger formed the okay signal, which was acknowledged by both George and Sherry who repeated the same sign confirming that they too were ready to go.

"Everyone ready?" Sunny boomed. "Okay, let's dive!"

With their mouthpieces locked firmly between their teeth, they stood and edged to the end of the platform. Putting one hand on his mask, Sunny entered the water first doing a textbook standing entry into the pitch-black water. He slightly inflated his jacket to give him buoyancy and waited for the others.

George and Sherry followed suit and were pleasantly surprised by the warmth of the water, which was now oozing inside their neoprene wet suits and gaining extra warmth from their own body heat. They finned over to Sunny who was hanging on to the marker buoy's anchor chain. Spitting out his mouthpiece, Sunny gave another quick bit of advice.

"Remember, stick close to me, and if anything bothers you at all, grab my leg."

They all indicated a further okay signal, then deflated the remaining air from their jackets letting their weight belts take effect and assist in a slow descent down the rusted anchor chain. With each passing meter, they felt the increase in pressure on their eardrums and periodically had to equalize the pressure by pinching their noses and blowing out, listening for the distinctive squeaky sound as their ears popped.

By now their flashlights were beginning to take effect as the wreck came closer. Brightly colored coral-encrusted shadows emerged, and as Sunny had

had said, the thought of any possible danger fizzled away as they became engrossed at the sight of the mighty *Thistlegorm*.

Sunny took them over the bridge area down to the number-two hold. This was considered the most interesting area of the wreck and was still in remarkably good condition.

The "tween deck," a shelf built within the hold to accommodate more storage space, came into view stacked with a number of World War II vehicles. Below them were still more vehicles, some of which were crammed with motorcycles on their backs. However, it was clearly evident that the past decade of tourist diving on the site had begun to take its toll. Divers searching for souvenirs had pillaged anything small enough to remove, despite the wreck site being designated as an official war grave.

It was a fascinating experience for the two novice divers, and George thought it was an excellent preparatory exercise for their main objective, which was now only a couple days away.

Sunny decided to cut the tour of the hold short and took them over the starboard side to the seabed, where lying alongside the *Thistlegorm* they came across one of the two steam engines destined for the

Egyptian Railway Company sitting upright in almost perfect condition.

When they squeezed into the driver's cabin, Sunny heard a feint whining sound as if a motorboat was on the surface. Thinking nothing of it he continued to show them the controls of the engine and its vast boiler which, when in use, would need a constant feed of coal from the neighboring tender, which was also still attached to the engine.

Just as they were about to disembark, a deafening sound, followed by an explosive after shock that almost pushed over the ten-ton locomotive sent them crashing against the side of the cabin wall. It was so heavy that Sherry was flung back into the coal tender and knocked semiunconscious. Fortunately, her second stage was still clamped between her teeth, and her breathing stayed regular.

Sunny quickly signaled to George indicating it was time to get back to the surface. Both rushed to Sherry to help carry her up, and it was then that Sunny noticed a shadow above. This was no ordinary beast; he immediately recognized it from the huge, rounded first dorsal fin and long, wide pectoral fins. It was a bronze color with a yellowish tinge and had a white belly and white tips on both the dorsal and pectoral fins. It was none other than Carcharhinus longimanus, otherwise known as the oceanic whitetip shark and a big mother too reaching over four meters. While probably not as scary as a Great White, this was a voracious specimen and probably accountable for more attacks on humans than any other species, particularly from shipwrecks.

Already the behavior of the shark showed aggressive undertones, and it was then that they suddenly realized they were not alone. Two more specimens arrived, this time young tiger sharks showing off their pale stripes and blunt noses with rows of razor-sharp, serrated teeth.

The situation was serious. How had they gotten there so quickly? What was attracting them? And what had caused that explosion? The trio was in trouble.

Beaver and his band of cohorts were up on the surface, which was now covered with blood and guts scooped out from the putrid drum, which Beaver was still emptying into the sea above what was left of the *Thistlegorm* wreck. As he touched the bottom of the drum with the scoop, Beaver decided it was time to hurl the remaining contents with the drum over the side as the stench was beginning to make him nauseous.

Jassim moored the boat next to Sunny Talal's boat and suggested Beaver and Harman get aboard and wait for half an hour, or the maximum amount of dive time left for the three divers if they were still alive. Jassim handed them a couple revolvers and a flare gun.

"Once you complete the job, fire off a flare, and I'll come and pick you up," Jassim said.

Harman was relieved to get off the small boat and board the bigger yacht, as having seen the size of the sharks in the water he noted that they were larger than Jassim's boat and had a horrible premonition of falling in and being eaten.

Beaver found the cooler on the flybridge and was already busy opening up one of the ice-cold Sakaras Sunny had stocked for the post-dive celebration.

"You know, this Egyptian beer isn't that bad. Come on up, and grab yourself a refreshment. I think this is going to be a long wait, as I don't reckon our friends likely survived the blast, let alone the feasting going on down below."

"Those creatures give me the shiver," Harman said accepting an opened beer.

Although Sunny had his harpoon, while it may have been effective against a solitary predator, it was not going to be of any help in this situation. It was a stroke of luck that they had left the wreck when they did as the locomotive had taken the brunt of the explosion. The number-two hold, where they had been, was devastated and resembled more the aft section that had been blown up by the Heinkel bombers. The bridge section, although badly battered, offered some protection and was still in easy reach of the anchor chain.

By now Sherry had returned to consciousness; however she was oblivious to what was going on. George put his arm around her in an effort to offer some comfort and shield her from seeing the circling elasmobranchs, which by now numbered more than half a dozen species.

Sunny pointed to the *Thistlegorm* and motioned that they should swim toward the wreck and use it as camouflage against the irritated sharks milling around.

One by one they swam quickly to the wreck, which now revealed fresh metal as a result of the blast.

While the sharks picked up on their trail as they finned rapidly away from the ghostly locomotive, it became clear that the sleek beasts were getting confused as they neared the wreck. This was due to a buildup in the magnetic field which, like interfering with a compass, affected the sharks' attack guidance system, a series of jelly-filled canals on their snouts, known as the ampullae of Lorenzini. On their final approach, sharks close their eyes with a protective membrane and rely on the ampullae to feed off bio-electric rhythms exuded by their prey; metal objects disrupt these signals, and this is why some sharks have taken bites from boat propellers. This was exactly the break Sunny had been hoping for and would give him a little more time to plan their next move.

Seconds passed like minutes, and minutes like hours as the three divers took refuge beneath the bridge section of *Thistlegorm*. In order to keep track of what was going on, they formed a circle, back-to-back, and kept the beams of their flashlights shining in all directions. The bronzed oceanic whitetip, although smaller than the adolescent tigers, proved more curious and darted toward the light, frenzied by the strong aroma of chum still languishing in the area.

Checking his dive computer Sunny noted that they only had about ten minutes left to make it back to the surface without having to make a decompression stop which, given the current circumstances, would be next to impossible. They would have to make a break soon, and in order to do this, some form of distraction would be needed to deviate the attention of the lurking predators, giving them time to shoot up to the platform and get out of the water.

Having dived with sharks for most of his life and heard the exploits of fellow divers and tourists, Sunny formulated a plan that would not involve the use of his harpoon, as he would never be able to guarantee firing off an effective shot, particularly in semidarkness. His plan would be simple, passing the harpoon to George. Sunny grabbed his knife waiting for the whitetip to make its next pass. As it reared over them, he thrust the knife into its pale-white belly. It reared violently, and with every thrash of its huge triangular tale, the razor-sharp knife slid down the length of its stomach, and as it pulled away, Sunny had to let go for fear of being carried away. Blood and viscera spewed out of the open wound, maddening the shark to such an extent that it started trying to gulp down its own entrails. The two tigers, as well as a number of reef sharks, homed in and sank their jaws into the massive animal pulling off chunks of flesh.

Sunny signaled to George and Sherry that this was the moment of truth and indicated to partially inflate their jackets so they could get to the surface, but they had to remember to blow out all the way up. Failure to exhale would cause their lungs to blow up like a balloon until the membranes burst, which could lead to an excruciating death. Still they had to risk it and get out of the water as soon as possible. Dropping their flashlights, the three shot up like rockets without looking at what was going on behind them. By luck, the boat's dive platform was still pointing in the right direction toward the anchor chain, and as soon as they were on the surface, they unbuckled their jackets to get rid of their tanks and make it easier to climb onto the platform. The darkness meant they could no longer see the melee that was happening all around them, but they could sense the rapid movements as the sharks darted to and fro picking up the remaining scraps of meat that littered the water. The fear of becoming another victim loomed in all their minds, and it took a great deal of will power to erase these thoughts and focus on getting out as quickly and quietly as possible. George was first up having already thrown the harpoon on deck. He quickly gave his hand to Sherry to pull her away from any prospective danger while Sunny brought up the rear. It was ironic that an oceanic whitetip that would normally make a meal of them had become a meal himself and given them an opportunity to escape.

George sensed something was wrong when he heard the distant whine of an outboard engine edging closer along with strange muttering coming from their own flybridge. George recognized the voice and grabbed the harpoon. With their black wet suits and neoprene socks, they made no sound as they climbed onto the main deck. George motioned to Sherry to hide below deck and wait for the all clear. Then George threw his weight belt over the side hoping to lure the two cockney hoodlums down from the flybridge.

Beaver got to his feet and looked over the side noticing a pale iridescence deep in the water that was formed from the lights abandoned in *Thistlegorm's* bridge.

"Oy, Harman. Go take a look, and see if you notice anything in the rear. I think Jassim must be on his way over to pick us up."

Harman, wanting to get away from Beaver's nonstop criticism, grabbed his revolver and made his way down to the main deck. Never considering that their quarry was already back on board waiting to intercept him at the stern end of the boat, well out of Beaver's earshot.

As Harman reached the steps leading down to the dive platform, he hesitated, still very wary of the encircling fins breaking on the moonlit surface and was totally unaware of Sunny, who by now had already drawn his dive knife from his ankle sheath and was approaching from the rear, his footsteps aptly cushioned by his neoprene bootees.

Sunny catapulted toward Harman and thrust the eight-inch, serrated blade deep into his side while grabbing the revolver from his hand. The blade, which had easily penetrated Harman's torso, passed between two ribs into the right lung, almost reaching his heart. With his respiratory system now seriously punctured, Harman started to cough violently and was unable to scream due to a mixture of blood, saliva, and bile filling up his oral cavity.

Sunny, still holding onto the hilt of the knife, gave Harman a massive push with his foot, sending his limp body over the rail onto the wooden dive platform.

"Harman! What's going on?" Beaver shouted.

Sunny leaped alongside Harman and rolled him into the blackened water.

With blood oozing from the knife wound, one of the frenzied tiger sharks picked up the scent and altered course keeping close to the surface so that Harman could see the telltale triangular dorsal fin heading straight for him.

Harman's eyes bulged with extreme fear, and with great effort he managed to let out one last scream. "Heeeelp meeeeeeeeeeeeee, Beeeeeaverrrr! Heeeeeeelp!"

Beaver jumped off the flybridge to find out what was happening. Leaning over the side he was horrified to see Harman's torso clamped in the mouth of a tiger shark trying to take chunks of flesh by snapping and using his tail to shake Harman from side to side like a rag doll.

Within seconds another shark took one of his legs, then yet another joined the party pulling the body apart almost as if it was being hung, drawn, and quartered all at once.

Beaver had never witnessed anything so terrifying and would not have wished such a death on anyone. The splashing sounds quickly petered out as the thrashing beasts gorged on the remnants of any leftover flesh and bone.

Still in a trance of disbelief and confusion, he heard the loud bang of Harman's revolver, which was now in Drake's able hands, and felt a sharp pain in his temple. Blood oozed out from Beaver's head and dripped onto the teak decks. He felt feint and nauseous having been heavily concussed by the bullet that had winged his skull. Dark clouds frosted over his eyes so he could hardly make out the outline of Sunny, Drake, and Sherifa.

"How did you make it?" he whispered struggling to get out the muffled words.

Not wanting to explain anything to the local authorities, Sunny pushed Beaver over the rail to join Harman as a dessert for the sharks.

"We must remove all evidence of their presence. George, you hose off the blood from the deck and dive platform. I'll get us away from here and alert the authorities about that mysterious drug smuggler's boat you thought you saw earlier. I suspect he's not far away, and it won't be too long before he comes looking for his friends. Tomorrow's divers will be in for a bit of a surprise, and we don't want to be around to face an accusations of demolishing one of Sinai's finest wreck sites!"

CHAPTER 12

Jassim wondered what had happened, as it was already more than an hour since he had left the two English ruffians to complete their objective, and he was getting concerned that no flare had been fired off to signal their pick up. Just as he was debating what to do next, he caught a crackle on the open radio channel and heard Sunny Talal speaking with the coast guard.

"Allah! Those bungling fools, what have they done? How could they have failed in what was such a simple task?" he muttered to himself.

He was going to have some explaining to do to bin Laden and did not relish the prospect of his wrath over this failure.

Not wanting to have any contact with the authorities now that the alarm had been raised, he decided it was best to head back to their Dahab base and avoid venturing anywhere near Sharm El-Sheikh, as they would no doubt be on the lookout for a boat fitting his description.

Just as a precaution, and probably more out of his own morbid curiosity, Jassim made a last-minute decision to quickly pass by the *Thistlegorm*'s marker buoy as Sunny Talal's boat by now had already weighed anchor and left.

As the silent v-hull slid toward the marker, Jassim turned on the forward spotlight and saw little evidence of any presence; however, just as he was about to change course and head back to Dahab, he caught a quick glimpse of a reflection on the water's surface that warranted closer inspection. As he approached the object, Jassim recognized it to be a body.

Beaver, awakened after being pushed into the cold sea, had luckily found a discarded buoyancy compensator that Drake had failed to recover after boarding the vessel. Having released the aluminum dive cylinder, he was then able to keep afloat and wait for someone to pick him up.

Grabbing a gaff Jassim hauled the body close and saw it was Beaver. Pulling him onto his boat, Jassim examined him more closely and noted that he had only suffered a relatively minor head wound, the bullet having creased his scalp causing two large flaps of skin to protrude as if it had been sliced open by a carving knife and which would need some stitching to prevent any further bleeding. The cold salt water had stemmed the flow of blood for the time being and caused it to turn whitish in color, but once his body warmed up, it would open up again.

Leaving Beaver perched to one side, propped against a couple of old, moldy, moth-eaten towels, Jassim decided to waste no further time with the wretch. He would leave him to either recover his strength or die, with the latter being the most likely option.

Jassim decided to head back to Dahab keeping as far from the coast as possible so that he could avoid any confrontation with the coast guard. All lights were out, and with its matte-black finish and silenced engines, the boat picked up speed leaving a wake that stretched back several kilometers before vanishing back into the open ocean.

That this simple plan had failed irritated him immensely, and as he pondered what he was going to say, he bit his nails as there was nothing else that could be done, and the more he thought about the repercussions the more nervous he became.

After about an hour of full throttle, Jassim heard Beaver cough and splutter.

"You might as well be dead. El Din is not going to take kindly to your incompetence!"

On that note, Jassim grasped his radio phone and contacted Selim bin Laden to debrief him on the night's events wondering what sort of backlash he would have to face over his failure to complete the operation.

As expected, he could almost feel the spittle as Salim exercised his wrath.

"Your bungling efforts are going to cost us dearly! Now the authorities are going to come down on us like a ton of bricks! We should never have trusted the English fools, as clearly they were incapable of handling such a task. What happened to them?"

Jassim said, "One likely ended up as shark bait, and the other's with me and needs medical attention when we get back to close off a head wound. How he survived with all those sharks around, Allah only knows."

"Get back here right away so we can decide how to clean up your mess and keep El Din pacified. I don't want to hear another word until I see you!"

Beaver had regained full consciousness and was moaning like a yeti in heat as his head throbbed intensely where the bullet had torn a three-inch gash just below his temple.

"I'm going to kill those bastards," Beaver muttered falling back into a trance.

Jassim decided this was the perfect time to take care of the stitching. Without a proper medical kit, he grabbed a basic needle and thread, which would have to do, and poured vodka over the wound in addition to the needle.

The pain must have been excruciating as Beaver immediately awoke when the alcohol penetrated his wound, and he let out a deafening roar.

As Jassim maneuvered the needle through the torn flaps of skin and pulled through the makeshift length of thread, fresh streams of blood oozed from the gash. Beaver moaned as if being tortured until he finally succumbed to delirium. Once the stitching was complete, Beaver looked like Boris Karloff's patched-up Frankenstein's monster. But at least he was still alive.

News of the failed mission traveled fast as bin Laden notified Mustafa El Din who called Johnston in London. Johnston was likewise furious.

"We mustn't lose our focus and need to get back in control of matters. Find out what their next move is!" he barked.

"Don't worry, my friend," El Din said, "we've been watching them closely and know what they're planning, as Drake has booked them on a flight to Luxor tomorrow morning, and I've made arrangements to have them followed and will also maintain a twenty-four-hour surveillance using my extensive network of spies. You mustn't forget that Luxor is my town, and no one can do anything there without me knowing about it!"

"Very well. I also intend to travel to Luxor and as soon as I can and will be based at the Valley of the Kings staying at the Hilton with my winter dig team. It will be imperative that we unravel the secret ahead of Drake so we can harvest whatever treasures may still be hidden! Mustafa, you'd better also keep the antiquities department well away, and muster up a loyal secondary dig team."

"It will be done, effendi," El Din replied. He put down the receiver and then radioed further instructions on to Selim who was by now at the Dahab base.

CHAPTER 13

As they pulled into their berth at Sharm El-Sheikh Harbor, Sunny suggested they could all do with another cold drink. He grabbed a can for himself and tossed the two remaining beers from his icebox to George and Sherry.

Recounting once again the events of the day Sunny remarked, "You guys certainly attract some interesting friends. Whatever you have planned for your ongoing trip, you'd better make sure you have some form of defense. The best I can do is make sure your dive knives are sharp enough, as that's pretty well all you can risk putting into your luggage for the flight along with the rest of the limited dive gear. Better not to create any fuss, and keep your heads down ."

"Thanks, Sunny. My hope is that we reach Kom Ombo before Johnston and his cronies, although

I have to assume they'll already be on to us bearing in mind all the ruckus from the last twenty-four hours. We definitely need to be as discrete as possible."

On leaving the boat, they blended well with all the other tourists on the pier for excursions and dives, and no one took notice of them as they made for the car.

Sunny's driver was already waiting to take them back to the Movenpick where they could shower and ready themselves for the next part of their journey.

Sunny announced he would prepare a dive bag and include two of the smaller Luxfer AL13 scuba tanks having assumed this should be good enough for a short and shallow dive. In addition to masks, fins, regulators, weights, and the compact Fenzy buoyancy compensators, he would also provide two small but powerful flashlights, not to mention the razor-sharp knives.

For the rest of the drive there was complete silence as they contemplated the next piece of the puzzle and thought about what the papyrus scroll was leading them into.

Back in the room, Sherry collapsed on the bed and started sobbing with a cascade of tears that caused her black mascara to stream down her sculptured cheeks. As the adrenalin rush of the past few hours came to an almost abrupt halt, her body adjusted back to a state of normality and lead into a state of post-traumatic stress.

"This is far more than I bargained for. I can't believe Johnston has resorted to this extreme behavior. I've never seen anyone die before, let alone eaten by sharks! It makes me wonder even more what you've stumbled across. Maybe Johnston has unraveled the puzzle?"

"You have a point there. He certainly seems to have stepped up his game, and we'll need to be more vigilant than ever and take nothing for granted as we move forward. While I know it's going to be very difficult, we should try and get some shut eye," George said with a sigh, while trying to comfort Sherry with a compassionate hug, knowing full well that the evening's escapade was going to make it very difficult, as well as the fact that their body clocks were completely out of synch. Nonetheless, it would do them well to get some rest.

George waited for Sherry to nod off, then decided to head for the Egypt Air counter in the hotel to collect their tickets for their flight to Luxor the next morning. He had also gotten the hotel front desk to book them a room at the Movenpick Crocodile Island, which they would use as a base camp, keeping well away from the Hilton, where he was supposed to be staying while exploring the Temple of Kom Ombo.

Returning back to the room, George woke Sherry and suggested they go and relax on the beach and shake off any remaining jittery memories of their earlier adventure.

"You know what they say, if you fall off a horse, you should get right back on it. The sea will be good for us and get our minds tuned back to the job at hand," George remarked.

"Well, at least I know there are no sharks near the shore, and we'll be a lot safer among the crowds of tourists," Sherry replied.

The chilled-out beach atmosphere proved to be just what the doctor ordered. Snorkeling among the coral reefs just a few meters off lush, golden sands, the sea was teaming with groups of sergeant majors, parrots, triggerfish, and many other exotic species. It was a fantastic distraction and brought back beaming smiles to their faces.

Once out of the water, and with the sun already past its midday peak, George decided it was time for another ice-cold Sakara. Perching themselves at the barasti-covered beach bar and savoring the cool golden nectar, they mulled over how they were going to penetrate the Kom Ombo temple without drawing any attention, as whatever the papyrus was leading them to, it was imperative that no one else knew what they were up to.

The rest of the day went by uneventfully, and by late afternoon, they thought it best to retreat to their room, watch some TV, and call it an early night.

Sunny, as promised, had dropped off the dive bag while they were on the beach, and they were now fully equipped to move on to Luxor.

George decided to get all the hotel-checkout formalities done before they bedded down for the night, as this would enable them to get up and leave without any bother.

The next morning, after having had a restless night in anticipation of the excitement that lay ahead, few words were exchanged as they readied for their journey.

The ride to the airport took only fifteen minutes, and because they were flying domestically, check-in formalities were equally as fast despite having to endure several body-search checks and baggage X-rays lines. Once in the departure lounge, they waited with a large group of Japanese tourists who were no doubt on their way to see the marvels of Luxor and the Valley of the Kings.

Once the flight was ready for boarding, they were all ushered onto an ageing bus and shuttled off to the Egypt Air Express Embracr aircraft that had earlier arrived from Cairo. The flight took off on schedule banking sharply to the left, providing stunning views of the coastline, coral reefs, and reems of hotels that stretched for miles all the way to the town of Sharm El-Sheikh and beyond. The crystal-clear waters of the Red Sea had a striking array of colors from the light turquoise of the shallows to a dark-Prussian blue as its depth increased.

CHAPTER 14

The flight was barely forty minutes and included a light snack consisting of a couple biscuits and a soft drink. On arrival, there was no passport control to endure, and all they needed was to wait for their baggage and look for a suitable car-rental place.

George left Sherry to retrieve the bags and headed for the Avis counter he had spotted at the other end of the baggage hall. Fortunately, they had an old two-door Jeep Wrangler in stock, which would be ideal for their jaunt. George snapped it up for a couple weeks, not knowing how long they were going to be there. After paying, he collected the keys and location details, then looked for Sherry, who was guarding their luggage on a rickety airport trolley.

There was only the one Jeep in the parking bay, so it was easy to spot and load up. Their ride to Crocodile Island was relatively short as Luxor, despite being a fairly significant city, was pretty compact. They drove past the magnificent Temples of Karnak and Luxor, which were extremely impressive, and noted that many of the houses and roads between the two sites were in the process of being demolished so the authorities could properly excavate the great avenue of sphinxes which stretched several kilometers and joined up the two historic temples with an estimated 1300-plus sphinxes, most of which were destroyed during the Roman occupation.

The room at the Movenpick was all ready for them, and they were greeted with the customary cold wet towel and glass of refreshing *karkadeh*, all of which made the environment very special. George also picked up a tourist guide that had a detailed history of all the main temples, although George was only really interested in learning more about Kom Ombo so they could study the layout and plan how to best execute their objective.

"Let's head out to the veranda overlooking the Nile for another refreshment and work out our plans for tomorrow. I think we should try and scope out the temple during the day and see if we can sneak back in once it closes and look for the next clue," George suggested.

"That sounds fine to me, and also I think the sooner we can get past this objective, the better, as maybe we won't find anything and can just take a short holiday here and enjoy each other's company while avoiding any further confrontations," Sherry replied with a grin.

"Umm, I'll definitely go right along with that! Tomorrow will be our D-Day and deciding moment! Come on, let's go. I'll take this guidebook along so we can run through every detail."

It was a short walk from their room to the veranda, and the view of the Nile from their table was spectacular. A few feluccas gracefully sailed up- and downstream adding to the picturesque backdrop, and in the distance they could see the pyramid-shaped peak that guarded the historic Valley of the Kings.

"What a view! I could look at this every day and feel like I'm in heaven! No wonder the ancient Egyptians revered this area and wanted it to be their final resting place," George added as he pulled out the guide and gave Sherry a quick synopsis, even though he was preaching to the converted. Sherry's knowledge of ancient-Egyptian temples was vastly superior to that of a tour guide. Nonetheless, she was very happy for George to refresh her memory.

Having ordered drinks from one of the neatly uniformed waiters, George started mulling over what they needed to do the following day. "Kom Ombo will be about a three-hour drive, as it's about two hundred kilometers from here. I suggest we try and leave around 8:00 a.m., which will get us there around eleven. We can then do a quick a reconnoiter and maybe join a guided tour to be less conspicuous. Fortunately, the temple is in ruins so security should be pretty limited, and there will be no tourists hanging around once it closes to the public at around five, and I imagine will also have little in terms of locals since it's a fairly remote spot?"

Grabbing his breath, George went on further recounting what he had just researched from a local guidebook: "As you already know, Kom Ombo, historically, is a temple structure that was built predominantly within the Ptolemaic period, so most of what remains postdates our papyrus. However, there are still a couple sections left which are of a much earlier period. We certainly know part of it was built by Thutmose III in honor of the crocodile god Sobek, and this will be the portion we're interested in, as it covers the New Kingdom era and fits relatively close to our timeline. I suspect these ancient structures were also added on to an earlier existing building fitting in nicely with our research. Thutmose III ruled between 1479 BC and 1425 BC, and his tomb in the Valley of the Kings is numbered KV34.

"It appears this older portion is centered around the remnants of a crocodile statue outside the main temple and close to the Nilometer, which directly links the temple with the Nile and was probably used as some form of flood gauge. This is where we need to don our dive gear and explore what lies beneath, according to your interpretation of the papyrus. If we don't find anything here, then it's game over. If I'm right, we may be able to access the Nile from the Nilometer and use this as our preferred exit point to minimize risk of discovery."

Sherry chuckled and nodded her approval. "Wow! You're certainly learning our history very fast and becoming quite the budding Egyptologist."

George scribbled some notes on the basic schematic of the temple within the guidebook and suggested parking the Jeep close to the Nile bank and near enough to the temple to not raise any suspicions. He once again briefed Sherry through the plan outline and how they could quickly gain access to the Nilometer under the cover of darkness without being spotted.

The Nilometer thankfully had a series of limestone steps leading down to the water level, although they might have to jump in from the last step, which would be only a few feet up. With this in mind, George suggested taking a short piece of rope, just in case they needed to exit from the point of entry if the Nile exit was blocked.

"Now we've got the plan set for tomorrow, so let's finish our drinks and do a little sightseeing or take a dip in the pool."

They settled for an afternoon swim as they preferred not to stray too far in advance of the long day ahead.

CHAPTER 15

Selim bin Laden and Beaver were making their way to Luxor to make contact with Johnston who was due to arrive that evening. They had decided to meet up at the Hilton Luxor shisha lounge at 10:00 p.m. allowing for any travel delays that night. El Din had already updated Selim knowing that their adversaries were staying at the Movenpick, as he was keeping tabs on their movements.

Wafts of sweet-smelling shisha smoke with mixed aromas of differing fruits, mint, and molasses filled the room with a smoggy atmosphere as an erotic belly dancer performed her routine, scantily clad with just a thin coin scarf around her hips matching coin-studded bikini top, which was barely enough to cover her buxom, bouncing breasts. With a transparent chiffon shawl adding to the erotica she encircled each table and demonstrated her skills of lifts and drops, twists and rapid undulations to the loud clamor of darbuka drums as she lightly brushed against each guest, inviting them to join her and imitate her almost impossible moves.

Johnston had by now arrived and joined Beaver and Selim for a shisha in one of the more secluded alcoves away from the loud music and dancing so they could discuss matters at hand.

A waiter dressed in a smart army-like uniform sporting the traditional red fez hat carried in three ornate glass-and-steel shishas. One by one he untangled each of the long, flexible, velvet-covered hoses and loaded their prefilled, foil-covered tobacco tops with red-hot wood charcoal. Using the bare hose end he then took a few strong puffs to make sure each was in good order before inserting the mouthpiece, handing over each of the pipes with an additional sterile plastic insert. As they sucked in the flavored smoke through the ornate water-filled vase, the telltale hubbly bubbly sound reverberated around them and kicked up a light-headed buzz.

Selim decided to break the ice. "Hey, we can get them to put a little hashish on top of the tobacco if you like, as I know they have some stashed away for VIPs."

Johnston was in no mood and got down to business. "I've been deliberating over how best to conduct this Drake matter and think we should let them finish whatever it is they're intending and only take decisive action once we know where X is on the map."

"Uh, what do ya mean?" Beaver replied while picking at a scab that was already beginning to manifest around the crude stitching on his forehead, his head still throbbing.

"You're even dumber than I thought, and if I'd known ahead how useless you would have performed in Sharm El-Sheikh, I never would have hired you. The loss of Harmon is probably a blessing, as having two of you idiots around would no doubt be a complete disaster. As Drake and the girl are still alive, I'll let them work for us and finish deciphering the scroll rather than doing it myself. It will be far easier to keep tabs on them, and when they eventually put the final piece of the puzzle together, you can then get rid of them both, comprendez!?"

"Yeah, boss! And sorry for screwing up the other day, it won't happen again," Beaver concluded sucking up another lungful of sweet smoke.

"Good, I'm glad we're all in agreement! Selim, you get your spies out there, and keep a close watch on Drake. Don't lose sight of them, as we need to see their every move."

The uniformed waiter passed by again, this time swinging a red-hot pot containing fresh charcoal and refreshed their shishas. Having placed the pot safely on the stone floor, he then removed the ceramic tobacco bowl and blew through it to clear it of any residual ash. Then, placing the bowl back on top of the stem, he added fresh charcoal on top of it, took the hose, having already removed the mouthpiece, and drew a few heavy puffs to make sure it was smoking perfectly before replacing the mouthpiece and handing it back. Having replenished their shishas, they then ordered a carafe of Lebanese arak with a bucket of ice and still water.

"Remember, keep me posted on a daily basis with *all* their moves!" Johnston said deciding not to stick around and headed for his room to get some rest.

Beaver and Selim finished all the arak and continued to smoke until they too decided it was time to retire back to his opulent safe house on the outskirts of Luxor.

Selim then called his contact at the Movenpick and found out that Drake and the girl were already in their room for the night but that they had requested a wake-up call for 6:30 a.m. Selim instructed his contact to continue watching them and that he would have a car pass by at around 7:00 a.m. to keep track of them if they left the premises.

CHAPTER 18

George awoke well in advance of the wake-up call. Having given the excursion more thought he decided it would probably be too long a drive to get back the same day, so as a precaution he booked a room at the Old Cataract Hotel in Aswan for a couple nights, as that was only a forty-five-minute drive from Kom Ombo and would give them time to take a break as well as plan what to do next.

He asked the front desk to make the booking for him and told them they would be back in two days and that they should keep their room blocked while they were away.

The request came as no surprise to Mohammed, who was manning the desk, as tourists often used Luxor as their base in Upper Egypt and would only make a quick trip to Aswan to see the monuments there. The Old Cataract Hotel was also a favorite having received its acclaim during the filming of Agatha Christie's *Death on the Nile*.

Mohammed gave a quick call to Selim and advised him of the latest change.

"Well done for letting me know right away. No need to follow them now, as we can save time and send our car down to Aswan to be waiting for them there!"

Selim then briefed Johnston who concurred with the plan and suggested Beaver join the driver and head over to the Old Cataract and ready himself for Drake's arrival.

Selim called Beaver and ordered him to get dressed and ready to move over to Aswan.

"I've asked the driver waiting at the Movenpick to come back here and take you to Aswan. We know Drake's next move, and rather than add to any altercation or arouse suspicion, we can head right to where they're booked to stay after their visit to Kom Ombo. When you get there book yourself a room at the Old Cataract and ask the concierge to let you know when they arrive. Give him some *baksheesh* and stress that it will be a surprise; he must not let them know of your presence!"

"Sounds good! I'll have to spruce myself up a bit to look the part, so let me get washed up, and maybe I can also stop by the shops and pick up some fresh clothes," Beaver said.

"Excellent idea! I'll give you ten thousand Egyptian pounds, which should cover all your expenses over the next few days, so spend it wisely; I will not be giving you any more money. Also, remember to call in on your arrival and confirm everything's in place. We certainly don't want to experience any more of the Johnston wrath!"

CHAPTER 17

The morning air was misty and remarkably chilled. In the distance, with the sun beginning to rise over the Valley of the Kings, there were a number of hot-air balloons drifting and providing spectacular views of the ancient temples and monuments. George parked himself at a breakfast table overlooking the Nile and waited for Sherry.

When she arrived, George briefed her about the slight change in plan.

Sherry grinned and exclaimed, "Wow! That's a great idea and could be a perfect end to all our endeavors, assuming we don't find anything, of course. It's truly a romantic setting, and I'm looking forward to sharing a few cocktails with you out on the veranda there, which is out of this world!"

While they ordered their breakfast of foul and *taamia* falafel with freshly baked traditional *aish baladi* (Egyptian bread), along with a pot of English breakfast tea, they decided to run through the plan for the day and their notes relative to the scroll's interpretation.

"From what I can remember and noted down after your deciphering of the hieroglyphics, once we've entered the crocodile pool and accessed the tunnel, which I believe should still be intact, we'll need to head around fifty paces inside, then start looking for the pharaoh's cartouche. Sounds too easy; however, even though it looks straightforward enough, no one checking out this obscure void would have thought anything was buried or hidden there. It will have been easily overlooked all these millennia, and the only clue that would have altered the cause was thankfully hidden away in my great-aunt's travel guide just for us!" George remarked taking Sherry's hand and giving it a gentle squeeze.

"I can't wait to get this over with. Let's head back to the room, pack an overnight bag, as you put the dive equipment in the back of the Jeep already, and get underway," Sherry added.

Having quickly stuffed an additional set of clothes into a small bag, along with their toiletries, they left the room, not forgetting to hang the housekeeping card on their door knob.

They took the scenic route passing through Edfu on the way down to Kom Ombo where there was another magnificent temple dedicated to Horus which sported the second-largest pylon in all of Egypt as well as a very well preserved sacred falcon colossus standing proudly at the entrance, as if guarding it from enemies.

Having agreed that it would be better not to waste any more time, they decided not to get out and to continue their journey all the way to Kom Ombo and only stopped once to fill up with gas and grab a cold drink. The whole journey took them nearly four hours in all including the stop, and by the time they reached the temple site it was already past midday.

Kom Ombo is home to only about 60,000 inhabitants and some fifty kilometers from Aswan, which is a much more significantly sized urban city with a population over 1.5 million.

The Temple of Kom Ombo was fortunately located a short distance out of town on a sharp bend of the Nile and nestled between strips of agricultural land being used to grow sugar cane so would certainly be easy to access once the sun went down. The only sign of life was a small electronics store a little further down river and not big enough to attract much activity.

On the riverbank in front of temple was a perfect spot to leave the Jeep only eighty meters from the Nilometer, and because of its fairly ruined state, there were not any security fences or walls present, so everything would be easily accessible.

George found an ideal spot and parked the car under some trees on the riverbank. Taking Sherry by the hand, they strolled over to the temple and paid a small fee at a basic kiosk near the temple entrance so they could walk around and case the area.

The temple itself was an interesting piece of architecture and unusual because of its double design due to the fact that it represented two gods, Sobek and Horus, with the latter also referencing Hathor and Khonsu. George needed no guide, as Sherry was able to give him the full rundown and also explain many of the intricate carvings, some of which illustrated how advanced they were scientifically at the time including one frieze which pictured an array of sophisticated medical instruments and another depicting the lunar calendar.

They then inspected the Nilometer, which was their prime target and one of the finest surviving examples in Egypt. The structure was extremely important for the well-being of the people at the time, as it was used to measure the depth of the river and used as a gauge to predict when the floods were due so they could accurately plan when to grow and harvest their crops.

Guarded by the nearby crocodile statue, or colossus, which was only really recognizable by its shape, having been heavily eroded by weather, the design layout was far better than expected, as the stairs leading down from ground level went all the way to the water's edge in a circular pattern and formed part of the wall of the Nilometer. At the bottom, some fifty feet down, was a pool of water resembling a stagnant well and probably full of mosquito larvae.

"That looks perfect, as we'll have no difficulty getting down to the water's edge without being noticed. Also, I wouldn't have liked to jump from any height in case it was too shallow. I suggest we take the bare minimum of equipment and only use our masks, tanks, and weight belts to get us down and, of course, our knives and torches. No need for fins and buoyancy compensators here. We can use the three millimeter wet suits to protect ourselves against rough edges or sharp objects, and their black color should help keep us camouflaged," George said.

"That makes perfect sense, and I'd suggest we jettison our tanks when we exit the river or leave them in the tunnel if we get out the way we entered. We won't have any further need of them," Sherry said, raising her cute eyebrows and signaling that she was also getting a little impatient now that they had wait for sundown. Let's find somewhere nearby to rest and come back later. We can leave the car here and walk downriver until we find a local restaurant, as there must be something nearer to town."

They walked hand in hand along the twisting bank of the Nile for a couple miles, and the few locals they passed en route took no notice. After half an hour they reached a local eatery and were able to sit down, relax, and grab a light bite, carefully selected by Sherry, and washed it down with a glass of Sakara.

After a while the sun began to wane, and George suggested walking back to the Jeep so they could kit up and ready themselves for a dash to the Nilometer.

As they strolled back to the temple area, they chatted through the action plan again and debated all the possible things that could go wrong, particularly if they were spotted and how to argue themselves out of what could be a very awkward predicament and probably something that would require a substantial amount of *baksheesh* to remedy.

On reaching their vehicle, George pulled out Sunny's dive bag, unzipped it, and emptied all the contents into the back of the Jeep. He then took the pair of Luxfer tanks and carefully fitted the second stage of their SCUBAPRO regulators to each tank, opened up the valves, and purged the second stage of each regulator to ensure they were working properly. The tanks were only thirteen inches long and at the minimal depth of the well held more than a sufficient amount of compressed air to last them, as at the very worst they would probably only need to swim fifty feet. They were also very light and would not be cumbersome when they made their hundred-meter dash across the open yard to the Nilometer.

Having checked out all their equipment, they stripped down to their bathing suits and donned the black wet suits, which were very welcome as the chilled desert night air had already began to give rise to goosebumps, and George chuckled as he noticed Sherry quickly zip up the front to hide her protruding nipples.

"You naughty man," she said beaming at him and knowing full well she was teasing him.

Once the wet suits were zipped up, they put on their bootees and strapped the sheaths containing the razor-sharp dive knives to their calves. They also fitted small weight belts to counteract the buoyancy of the neoprene and held on to their flashlights, which were attached to their hands with wrist ties.

The temple courtyard was now in complete darkness and void of people. Fortunately, there was also no moon present meaning they would have a little bit of extra darkness to hide them when they finally made their run for the well.

Taking hold of their masks they decided that now was as good as ever to make their way over to the Nilometer. Their tanks had already been secured to lightweight back harnesses, which were also easy to carry using the grab handles located by the second-stage valve.

They crossed the road over to the temple courtyard, then sprinted to the well, not wanting to spend any time in the open. They descended down the inner stone stairway, all the way to the water's edge almost fifty feet from the surface. Now totally concealed, they helped each other fit their tanks onto their backs and decided only to use their flashlights once they were underwater to further limit any signs of their presence. George also had a lightweight, waterproof goody bag, just in case they found anything of interest that needed sealing.

"Are you ready?" whispered George. "Let me get in first, then you follow. I'll grab the bottom step and wait for you. Once you're beside me, we can sink to the bottom and start looking for the tunnel entrance. Remember, if you encounter any difficulty, you can always unclip your weight belt and return to the surface. We can switch on our torches at the bottom."

With her regulator already in her mouth, Sherry gave him the okay signal and waited for him to enter the water, which he did very gently, again trying to keep noise to a minimum. Sherry then followed suit.

Letting go of the step, they both sank to the bottom of the pool, which was only about another fifteen feet. It was pitch black, and even when they switched on their flashlights, the visibility was poor. Stone slabs that had long ago formed part of the main structure littered the floor, and that they were covered in mud and slime made it very difficult to maneuver around. The well would have originally been enclosed within its own building and would no doubt have been an impressive sight. In the middle of the well would have stood a stone pillar with ornate engravings marking all the important levels, the lowest being hunger, with additional lines to represent other key characteristics of the Nile's water level from suffering to happiness to security to abundance with the highest level labeled disaster.

Within a few minutes grappling around the wall, George found the hollowed-out arch, which led to the tunnel, and gestured to Sherry to follow him. After negotiating a few more fallen limestone slabs there was another stairwell, which they then traversed and surfaced into what was clearly the tunnel referenced on the scroll and which at the time of the pharaoh would have been likely accessible from another entrance long since blocked off.

There was no decoration evident, as during times of flood this tunnel would have also been completely submerged, and it was no doubt there to allow for the Nilometer to be properly maintained and perform any repairs to the flood chamber.

Sherry removed her regulator from her mouth and took a breath of the air in the tunnel, which was breathable and hopefully free of pathogens.

"Wow! This is amazing. I think all we need to do now is take fifty paces from the top of the steps and start looking for a cartouche," Sherry said getting ready to start counting her steps.

"Wait. I'll do it too, as we don't know how tall the guy was, so it could be anywhere in the area surrounding our marker points," George said, also buzzing with a shot of adrenalin.

They counted their paces, and on reaching the end found themselves separated by about three meters.

"Okay, this is the area we should start investigating. Use your knife to expose any points of interest, as it looks like they've used bricks for the walls of the tunnel, all of which are fairly weathered with erosion over the millennia, so we might be looking for a needle in haystack. You take the left side, and I'll do the right, then we can reverse if necessary and try again."

The walls were encrusted with mud and dirt, so it was not going to be an easy task, and after over an hour of searching the small target area they had still not located anything to warrant further investigation and were wondering if they had gotten their measurements wrong.

Just as they were about to give in, George's flashlight caught a faint shadow of an outline in one of the bricks, which looked as if it could have been some ancient graffiti. Taking out his knife, he scraped off the dirt, and there in front of him, he could see the markings of a cartouche, which was probably missing a few of the images and less than half of the complete script.

"Check this out, Sherry, and see if you can interpret any of the characters."

Sherry shone her flashlight onto the exposed markings and made out a few of the letters, the twisted wick of an *h* followed by a chick representing an *o* and a bit further down an owl which sounded out an *m*.

"This looks very promising, and I think we've got it," Sherry exclaimed.

George took his knife and started to dig out the dirt and grout surrounding the graffitied brick, and as more of the dirt was removed he could sense the brick getting looser. By now he could sink his knife almost six inches into the wall all around the brick.

"Quick, get your knife, and wedge it in the bottom as far as possible. I'll do the same to the top of the brick, then let me take hold of both knives, and I'll see if I can yank it out without breaking our blades."

With both knives now firmly in place, George carefully levered them in an up-and-down motion, slowly first, then to get more movement driving the hilts deeper into the wall. With the stone now clamped between the two knives, he started to pull them back very mindfully, and as he did so, the brick began to move in synch emerging out of its cavity. Once the brick was exposed by a few inches, George took out the knives and grabbed onto the brick pulling it with his MIGHT. Slowly but surely it began to move more and more until it eventually slid out.

Dropping the brick to the floor, he then shone his flashlight into the hole to get a closer look at what had hopefully been hidden there. There, at the back of the cavity, was a small ceramic jar still intact and sealed, which George removed and handed over to Sherry.

"This is mind-blowing, and I almost feel we're stealing one of our ancient treasures. We must handle this really discretely and be mindful not to destroy anything, as one day it will no doubt be a museum piece."

"I agree, and the sooner we can check out what's in this pot and photograph the content, we can put it away somewhere safe and hand it over to the antiquities department when the time is right. In the meantime, we have a mystery to unravel!" George said while unzipping his waterproof goody bag.

"Give it to me, and I'll guard it with my life."

George took the jar and sealed it into the waterproof recovery bag and motioned that they should start thinking about getting back. Taking the lead, he said, "Let's get to the end of the tunnel and see if we can exit by the river."

The channel he knew would undoubtedly connect somewhere with the Nile and estimated that they were probably about another hundred meters or so from the riverbank, wherever that might be. As they moved on, the tunnel roof began to get lower and lower, and as they approached the end of the passage, there were more steps leading down to the water's edge.

Before reaching the steps, George noticed what looked like squiggly lines in the muddy sand in front of them and pulled Sherry over toward him, knowing full well that something was not quite right, as he also glimpsed the outline of a large serpent-like creature rearing up.

Shining his flashlight in the direction of the snake, Sherry recognized the species.

"Hell, I think we have a slight problem ahead," George said.

"Absolutely," Sherry whispered. "We need to be very careful not to get too close to it. This is a very large and dangerous snake. It's an Egyptian cobra, and out here, we probably wouldn't survive long if one of us got bitten. The venom is a highly potent neurotoxin and would likely interfere with the heart muscles and lead to respiratory failure. Remember Cleopatra!"

"I think we should head on, bypass it, and hope there aren't any more once we hit the water," George suggested, not wanting to turn back.

By now the cobra was clearly visible and probably an adult measuring some two meters in length. Coiled up and ready to strike, its large head had already reared up over two feet from the ground, and to demonstrate it really meant business, it fanned out its hood and arched back in defiance. The creature's beady pupils glowed in the dark reflecting back their flashlight, and its signature tear-drop markings were clearly evident under each eye.

Remaining still, George said he had an idea how to keep it pinned down so they could make a break for the water. "We both still have a reserve octopus attached to our regulators so we really only need one bottle between us. If you give me yours, I can detach the first stage, open up the air, and throw it on the ground near the snake. It will at the very least make him head in the opposite direction, and we can hit the water and squeeze ourselves through the remainder of the tunnel with you sharing my air supply. We'll need to be quick, as I don't know how long the noisy air distraction will last as these are small tanks."

Sherry turned around slowly so George could unhitch her tank and remove the first stage. Keeping his eye on the cobra, he then tossed her regulator in the opposite direction and quickly opened up the main valve to release the remaining high-pressure air supply into the atmosphere. In the confines of the tunnel, the noise was deafening. He then threw the tank on the ground in front of the snake, which by now was petrified and slithered away deeper into the tunnel. Not knowing how long the distraction would last, George took Sherry's hand.

"Quick, let's get out of here!"

"Okay, I'm ready and will hang on to you somehow," Sherry said biting onto George's octopus second-stage mouthpiece and giving it a quick purge to get the air flowing.

The exit was extremely narrow, almost like a sewerage pipe, and very claustrophobic, still neatly bricked by the same sort of limestone slabs but covered in weeds, reeds, and papyrus plants making it invisible from the bank. They had to use their knives to clear some of the reeds, and when they eventually emerged and surfaced by the riverbank, they were only a few meters away from their Jeep.

"Wow, that was quite a scary exit! Let's get out of these clothes and skedaddle quick, as I'm beginning to feel drained from all this excitement."

The crusty remnants of dirty Nile water, which by now had dried on to their skin, would not smell particularly good under their clothing, nevertheless, a hot shower once they got to the hotel would remove all evidence of this, and hopefully neither of them had picked up any waterborne diseases common to the Nile, such as typhoid or legionnaires.

George placed his goody bag containing the ancient jar into their overnight bag, then repacked the dive bag with all their equipment including the remaining scuba tank, which he had previously thought of dispensing with. He then settled into the driver's seat and motioned to Sherry to climb in and buckle up.

Leaving Kom Ombo without any incident was a great relief, and the drive to Aswan only took them another forty minutes. By the time they pulled up at the hotel-lobby entrance, it was after midnight, and they welcomed the fact that the car would be valet parked.

While checking in, George clung to his overnight bag, not wanting to hand it over to any porter, and strolled into the lobby. After signing the register and leaving their passports at the front desk, they took the elevator to the third floor and ambled over to their room, 308.

Despite the fact that they were almost beyond total exhaustion, they removed all their clothes, dumped them on the floor, and made for the en-suite bathroom, hand in hand. George then ushered Sherry into the large walk-in shower and joined her. Within seconds, the glass door misted up as steamy hot water gushed out of a gigantic rain shower head and pelted their bodies with a blast of clean water, which they relished, sighing in bliss. After a couple minutes of soaking in the rainfall, they washed each other with the hotel-provided liquid soap and shampoo getting rid of all the grime that had been plastered on their bodies following the earlier excursion. George wrapped his arms around Sherry and hugged her letting the water continue soaking them and feeling her soft, clean, silky skin. Giving her a large kiss, he switched off the water and handed her one of the soft Egyptian-cotton towels that were neatly folded and stored on a shelf at the far side of the shower, sheltered from the spray area. Grabbing another towel, he rubbed himself down and wrapped it around his muscular torso following Sherry back out into the bedroom. Wasting no time and desperately in need of each other, they once again had earth-shattering sex, both wondering from where they had drummed up the energy.

"That was heaven," George whispered giving Sherry another kiss on her bronzed shoulder and cuddling her as if they were teenage lovers.

Opening up the minibar, George took out two bottles of Siwa mineral water handing one to Sherry and then indulging her with a history of the hotel, which he had researched when making his booking from Luxor.

"It may not surprise you, but I wouldn't mind betting that my great-aunt may well have stayed in this very hotel during her visit at the turn of the century and probably even read though her guidebook while sipping a gin and tonic and overlooking the Nile. Believe it or not, the hotel was coincidentally built by Thomas Cook in 1899 and has been a popular retreat for many well-known personalities including Winston Churchill, Tsar Nicolas II, Princess Di, and many other world leaders and royalty! Agatha Christie, not surprisingly, also stayed here and no doubt would have penned her Hercule Poirot crime novel *Death on the Nile* here."

"That's so interesting, darling, and you certainly do your homework, but, shouldn't we just take a quick peak inside the jar and see what it's hiding? I can't believe we've been holding back all this time, especially after all we've been through today," Sherry pleaded.

"It's been hidden away for over three thousand years, so one more night won't make a difference. We really need to have some natural light to be able to look at it properly. Remember, we'll need to be extra careful removing the contents, and I don't trust ourselves doing this properly in our current catatonic state."

"You're probably right. Let's get under those crispy sheets and get some shut-eye."

George unpacked what remained in the overnight bag, including the sealed ceramic jar, which he carefully placed in the drawer next to his bedside. Before climbing into bed, he sprinted over to the door, opened it, and placed the "Do Not Disturb" hanger on the door knob. Once the door swung back closed, he double locked it, and just for added security slotted the safety chain into position. Returning back to bed, he shut off all the lights and gave a passionate hug to Sherry, and soon they fell into a deep slumber.

Just across the corridor, in room 309, Beaver was already fast asleep, snoring heavily, having treated himself to a few too many sundowners earlier that day. The boredom of waiting had frustrated him, and he'd had nothing better to do than settle down on the famous veranda and sink pint after pint of the cool amber liquid, contemplating what his next move should be. On arrival at the hotel earlier that afternoon, he had made sure that his room was as close as possible to Drake's and informed Selim by phone once he had settled in.

The ornate open-air wooden gallery was neatly perched on a pink granite cliff overlooking the bank of the Nile and Elephantine Island just downstream from the first cataract, a narrow stretch of waterfall and rapids that began cutting through the valley or the world's longest river at Aswan, providing a spectacular view. In the distance, settled among sand dunes and palm trees, he could also make out the dome of the Aga Khan III Mausoleum, which was built in the style of a Fatmid tomb, not that he had any inclining of what it represented.

Selim had given instructions not to take any action for now and just keep a tight surveillance on the couple and watch their every move.

CHAPTER 18

George and Sherry awoke early the next morning full of excitement in anticipation of opening the jar and examining what it contained, wondering if anything had managed to survive all these years being stashed away behind the walls of the Nilometer for over three thousand years.

They ordered tea and croissants, which were delivered to them by an efficient and effusive room-service waiter whom George then generously overtipped.

Having wolfed down the pastries and washed them down with a couple cups of English breakfast tea, George cleared the tray from their table and left it on the floor in the corridor, just outside the door. He then decided that now was the perfect time to unravel the jar's secret.

Taking the ancient container from his bedside drawer, he placed it on the table and gestured Sherry to sit down next to him. As they looked down at the jar on the wooden table, they pondered how their world had so dramatically changed in just a matter of a few days.

The length of the jar was only about eighteen inches. It had a fairly wide neck, some two inches in diameter, with the rest of the earthen vessel around five inches diameter and weighed around one kilo.

"I have a camera in my bag, so I think it would be wise if we try and document everything when we open it, just in case anything gets damaged," George suggested.

"Good idea. I'll fetch it and be the official photographer."

Sherry took a couple pictures of George posing with the jar and waited for him to remove the seal.

Looking up at Sherry, George added, "I think we may need a small knife or something sharp to scrape out the seal. Do you have anything that might do the trick?"

"I can either retrieve one of the knives from our breakfast tray outside the room, if they haven't already removed it, or I think I may have a small metal nail file in my bag."

"Oh, yes! The nail file would be absolutely perfect."

Sherry grabbed her bag, opened it, and started rummaging through all the zipped pockets until she found her small makeup kit, which contained the file. Then she handed the small tool over to George who excitedly started working it into the seal, pushing hard, then swiveling it in a circular motion. Fragments of whatever dried sealant wax had been used to protect the contents began to litter the table along with copious amounts of fine dust.

"Try not to breathe in any of this, as it may not be too healthy," George remarked and suggested Sherry get the trash can and use a damp towel to clean up the mess.

After a couple minutes of scraping out the neck of the jar and removing all the dusty fallout, George felt the file give and sail through into the now open space within. With his fingers, he smoothed out the rest of the exposed orifice, turned it over, and gently shook it waiting for the contents to emerge.

The dried-up leather cocoon that had for so many millennia encased Siptah's scrolls, suddenly appeared, and as it emerged, George painstakingly took hold of it using just his thumb and forefinger and doggedly plied it out carefully placing the now empty vessel on to their bed.

After photographing the wrinkled sleeve, George decided it would be safe to remove the brittle leather encasement and try to examine the inner contents.

Still using the metal file, he cut through the delicate papyrus thread that had been used to secure the covering. He then peeled off the parched leather epidermis to reveal a number of scrolls, which were all in surprisingly good condition.

"What shall we do with these? I don't want to crack or break them if we try to unroll them," George said, knowing that Sherry had had a lot of experience handling similar documents during her stint with the Ministry of Antiquities.

"We need to get that papyrus a little moist. Run the shower for a few minutes with hot water only, which should, at least judging from last night's romantic encounter, be able to steam up the cubicle. We can then rest the scrolls on a chair in the steam for a few minutes so they can absorb some of the moisture, then straighten them out on the table."

"Sounds good to me," George said, and he undertook the task.

Once the scrolls were moistened, using a small napkin, George gently uncurled the ancient parchments making sure there was no damage to the papyrus or ink, separating them one by one from the overall bunch and weighing them down methodically using the corners so they could safely photograph them.

There were a total of three separate documents, and each contained rows of hieroglyphics that to George meant absolutely nothing, and he would have to defer now to Sherry to interpret them. She would be in her element, as this was exactly what she had trained to do.

Having photographed each one, George decided to try and get their film developed right away keeping his fingers crossed that the content wouldn't be looked at too closely. He had already ascertained that the hotel had a very small cluster of shops in the new wing, one of which was a photography outlet.

"Can I leave you for a short while to drop off the film for processing downstairs? You can work from the originals for now."

"Sure, I'll be happy to sit here and jot down some notes," Sherry said.

"Great, back in a tick."

Making his way downstairs and over to the new wing, George was unaware that he was being observed by Beaver who had heard the opposite bedroom door close signaling it was time to do a little snooping.

Instead of taking the elevator and risking discovery, Beaver raced down the stairs so he could pick up and dodge his quarry in the lobby area. He watched George head for the little shopping plaza and saw him enter the photo mart and hand over a roll of film for processing. He would wait for George to exit and return to his room before moving in.

With the coast clear, Beaver made for the photo-shop attendant and asked if he could use his telephone. Dialing Selim, he quickly explained where he was and asked if he could persuade the photo shop to make a duplicate set of the pictures from George's roll of film.

"This is an excellent bit of thinking, as it could make our job a lot easier this time round," Selim boomed. "Hand over the receiver to the man in the shop, and let me explain what we need him to do, and when I've finished give him two hundred pounds."

Beaver handed the phone over to the nervous-looking man and gestured for him to speak with

Selim who could converse with him in Arabic and firmly advise him that it was not only in his best interest to comply but also for the sake of his family's safety to make the duplicate set of photographs for Beaver to collect later on. Once the exchange was done, the man handed back the receiver to Beaver.

"He understands very clearly what he needs to do. Now go back to your room, and make sure you keep out of sight! Give me a call once you get the set of photographs, and we can then discuss our next steps."

The shop attendant looked pretty shaken up as Beaver handed him two crisp hundred-pound notes, and then he left the shop and headed back to his room.

George, in the meantime, had picked up a touristy, leather-bound folder from a souvenir shop in the lobby, inscribed with ancient-Egyptian symbols, as he thought this would be ideal for storing the original papyrus documents and keep them safely compressed. It would also serve to disguise the content, as no one would ever give it a second thought.

Back in their room, George found Sherry still leaning over the table studying all the papyrus symbols and scribbling an array of precise notes while attempting to put the jigsaw together on hotel stationary.

"What have you established so far?" George inquired.

"Well, from what I can see, this document was written by a high priest called Siptah, and it appears to be some form of revelation concerning the death of a powerful king named Horemosis whose cartouche we also discovered on the wall of the Nilometer in Kom Ombo. This would truly be an amazing discovery, as there is, as far as I know, absolutely no recording of this king at all in Egyptian history. I estimate he would have lived some time at the end of the Middle Kingdom or beginning of the New Kingdom, and that would place him somewhere in the Seventeenth to Eighteenth Dynasties or, to give you a better perspective, he probably would have ruled between 1600 BC and 1550 BC."

Sherry continued to brief George, and while in the middle of recounting her interpretation of the documents, she gave him a massive hug. Unable to contain her excitement, she became so emotional and almost powerless to believe that this gorgeous new man in her life was about to unearth one of her country's most treasured possessions.

"The way it's been written is very confusing and full of riddles. The writer almost seems to be afraid of recording the timeline of events, and I suspect all subsequent references to the pharaoh will no doubt have been wiped away, which is why we know so little about this era. The difference between the seventeenth and eighteenth dynastic rulers is quite remarkable in terms of advancements in all walks of life, so it would most definitely be a significant discovery if we can analyze this and maybe establish where this Horemosis is lying. The treasures could possibly surpass those of Tutankhamun and make the pioneering archeologist who finds him even more of a celebrity than Howard Carter was in 1922!"

"That's a thrilling prospect, and let's put it into better context, as it won't be a single celebrity but two celebrities!" George exclaimed, happily returning Sherry's hug.

"I think we should put the scrolls in the room safe for now and go downstairs. It would be good to get some fresh air out on the veranda as we can also pick up our snaps from the photographic shop on the way and take them with us. They should have been processed by now, as I recall the man did say it would only take about an hour to do the job, even though we asked for slightly bigger prints."

"My back's killing me from leaning over this table. Great suggestion, by the way."

"Hey, I forgot to show you what I picked up while I was downstairs." George showed Sherry the ornate leather folder, which also contained a cheap writing pad and matching pharaonic pen. Removing the notebook and pen, George meticulously secured the three papyrus scrolls into one of the document sleeves and locked it in their room safe.

Downstairs, the lobby was bustling with activity, as a tour bus had just arrived with another batch of tourists who were congregating near the check-in desk.

George took Sherry with him to the photo shop and let her do the talking. Speaking in Arabic, she went through all the usual pleasantries and even talked about where she was from in Egypt before asking for their photographs. The man, who was wearing a colorful traditional galabia, went to the back room and returned with an envelope containing all their prints, as well as the negatives, and included a fresh complimentary film cartridge.

"Elf shukre," Sherry said, thanking him for his kindness. She handed him fifty Egyptian pounds for doing the job and a twenty-pound tip.

As they were about to leave, the man spoke a few more words to Sherry. After they had both exchanged their salams Sherry slipped him a further two hundred pounds.

Outside the shop, George took hold of Sherry and whispered in her ear.

"What was all that about?"

"Let's not chat about this now. Let's get to the veranda, as I think I could do with a stiff G and T," Sherry muttered.

"Oh my god, you have me in complete suspense now," George said.

The two made a quick dash for the veranda and grabbed a couple relaxing wicker chairs in a quiet alcove overlooking the Nile.

"I think we may have been a bit too unwitting in thinking we were totally ahead of the game. The man in the shop asked me not to repeat what I'm about to tell you, as both his life and the lives of his family member could be at stake, but he was keen to earn an additional bonus!"

"Shit! You have my complete attention, and absolutely, we would never do such a thing. Go on," George said, extremely perturbed about their future predicament.

Sherry went into more detail. "It seems after you dropped off the film, you were followed by another English guy who had a large scar on his head. The dude then got him to speak with an Egyptian chap on the phone who threatened both him and his family. He instructed him to make duplicates of all our photos and give them to the bozo in front of him or face his wrath. Added to that, he was specifically told not to tell you what had happened…or else."

"I don't usually swear, but fuck, we've been snookered!" George said. "It must be the same guys that followed us all the way from London and blew up the *Thistlegorm* in Sharm! It sounds like your friend Mr. Johnston has got a lot of muscle over here, and we shouldn't underestimate him. Scarface is most certainly one of the two guys who chased us round the Tower and is turning out to be a real pain in the backside!"

George called over a waiter and ordered two large Bombay Sapphire gin and tonics with a dash of Angostura bitter, which he knew Sherry also liked, being her late maternal grandfather's favorite drink. Not being one to consume much alcohol, he remembered her telling him that she used to have a gin and tonic on the odd occasion when visiting her family home nestled opposite the Suez Canal in Port Saiid.

After the drinks arrived, George pondered what they should do next.

"Well, if Johnston gets hold of our photographs, how long do you think it will take him to get all the hieroglyphics interpreted, as we no longer have our head start over them?"

Sipping the sour but very refreshing liquid, Sherry deliberated.

"Well, two things stand out to me. For starters, I think we should cut back our stay here in Aswan and get back to Luxor as soon as we can, as we've done about as much as we can here. Secondly, we may still have the edge on deciphering the scrolls. There are few trustworthy persons that Johnston will be able to get under his wing and do the job without alerting the antiquities department, as I feel sure he'll want to access the tomb in advance of using any official channel and steal as much as he can of whatever treasure lies there. As I mentioned back in the room, the text was written in sort of conundrums, and it will not translate literally. We need to try and get into Siptah's head as we did with your great-aunt's scroll, albeit much simpler, and work out the true interpretation. Given all that, maybe we'll at least have a week's head start or maybe only a few days."

"Absolutely!" George agreed. "After our drinks here, and possibly a quick bite to eat, let's head back to the room and pack, check out, and return to the Movenpick in Luxor. Let's also assume we're being followed all the time now and always, so if we need to do something without giving away too much, try and shake off whoever it is that's following us before taking any action. Finally, let's avoid planning anything directly using the hotel or phones or any other third party, as we must assume Johnston has an exhaustive network of spies all over the place. I know we could probably kill everything off by making a direct approach to the antiquities department; however, we don't know how corrupt they are or if they're in cahoots with Johnston. Besides, we'd almost certainly lose our shot at unearthing this once-in-a-lifetime mystery, not to mention handing over all our hard work on a silver platter. As such, we need to try and do this alone, which will be difficult, particularly if we need to rely on any sort of excavation team."

Staring out at the beautiful backdrop and sucking in all the historical sites around them, George sighed, as he had actually been looking forward to checking out some of the ancient monuments around Aswan, such as the Unfinished Obelisk and also taking quick look at the High Dam, which now served as one of the major power sources for the whole nation. The dam also would have served to eliminate all the crocodiles that had historically swam in these waters.

George ordered some snacks for them and another round of drinks before closing the bill.

When they returned to their room, they were relieved to see that the folder containing the original scrolls had not been taken out of the safe. Having concluded that these documents were probably superfluous by now and of no further interest (other than the fact that they were no doubt of reasonable value), they got on with packing their meagre belongings, including the now empty porcelain jar. It hardly took any time to stuff their overnight bags, and within a couple minutes, they were once again walking back down to the lobby and checking out.

After settling the bill George noticed the office manager make a quick call and presumed he was notifying someone of their departure.

George's perception was correct, as the office manager had made a call to room 309 and tipped off Beaver that the couple had just checked out and were returning to Luxor. Beaver, by now, had already collected the duplicate set of images from the photo shop and had examined them before updating Selim. Selim had instructed him to sit tight until Drake and the girl left their room, and once they had checked out, for him to get back to Luxor as soon as possible. It was clearly a race now to see who would crack the coded message detailed on the scrolls, and he wanted Johnston to see the pictures without further delay, thinking he could outsmart their quarry and finish this jaunt once and for all.

CHAPTER 19

Tipping the valet driver, who politely opened the passenger door for Sherry to climb aboard, George slid into the driver's seat of their now dusty Wrangler, pushed the gearshift into drive, and pulled away. Leaving the spectacular pink colonial structure behind them, George relayed to Sherry that he was going to avoid the scenic route this time and instead of taking the M75 back via Kom Ombo and Edfu, he would head for the expressway on the west bank, which would cut almost an hour off their journey.

While George drove, Sherry opened the envelope containing all their photographs and also her rough transcripts of several sections of the archaic script. Attempting to extricate more secrets from the glossy prints, and the amazing story that was now beginning to unfold, she jotted down some additional, but this time noticeably squiggly due to the movement of the car, notes and immersed herself in the beautifully hand-drawn glyphs and imagined the scene that Siptah was recounting. It was as if she was with him.

The exhilaration she experienced stimulated her adrenal glands into action, adding further shots of adrenalin to what was already coursing through her veins. The will to untangle this narrative, and ultimately try to solve the impending mystery, was now turning out to be a real adventure and became even more pressing.

Turning to George, who was now completely focused on the road, she began to throw more light on some of the drawings and was really enjoying being part of Team Drake, and her dialogue began to hasten with all the exhilaration.

"George, honey, I can see that there's another cartouche drawn alongside that of Horemosis and feel this must be making reference to his queen, and her name, coincidentally, is the same as that of another future queen from the Eighteenth Dynasty, namely that of Hatshepsut, who ruled from around 1479 BC for some twenty-two years and was only the second recorded female pharaoh ever to reign. I think there must be some form of link here, as it would be far too much of a fluke to be anything otherwise. Incidentally, the Hatshepsut from the Eighteenth Dynasty was one of Egypt's great builders, and if we can steal a few moments back in Luxor, I'd love to show you her breathtaking temple, which is also pretty close to the Valley of the Kings. There is still quite a lot of mystery about this queen, as most of her memory, cartouches, and statues commemorating all her life and achievements were erased by her successors, and for a long time we were unaware of her significant importance, leading to what Egyptologists often referred to as the 'Hatshepsut problem.' Howard Carter discovered her tomb numbered KV60 back in 1903, around the time your great-aunt was also touring the region."

"That is interesting, and yes, I'd love you to show me the temple, maybe after we solve this puzzle, and maybe you could extend the tour to cover all the other areas of interest and more, if you get my drift," George added playfully.

Sherry knew what he meant and smiled back. She gave George's hand that was resting on the gearshift a quick squeeze.

Returning back to her scribbled notes and pulling out another glossy snapshot, Sherry drifted into an almost hypnotic stasis once again as she began to submerge deep into the images of their prized manuscript. The feeling she was experiencing was almost intoxicating, and the desire to unravel this mystery intensified by the minute.

George, meanwhile, had turned the radio on so he could have a little background music to keep him alert, as there was not much to look at outside the car, other than an arid desert landscape which had a somewhat soporific effect.

After more than three and half hours of nonstop driving, George made the home stretch, and with much relief, he maneuvered their Jeep up the long driveway and back in front of their hotel on Crocodile Island. He was exceedingly glad to get out of the vehicle and stretch his aching legs and also make a dash for the restroom to relieve his full-to-bursting bladder.

Sherry was also glad to have an opportunity to freshen up in the neighboring restroom, apply some bright, fresh lipstick to highlight her stunning Mediterranean tan, and also to spray on a little extra sweet-smelling perfume. George waited for her in the lobby, and when she was finally ready, they made their way, arm in arm, back to their room.

Beaver was also on his way back to Luxor having waited for Drake and the girl to leave first as instructed by Selim. He was desperately looking forward to handing over the photographs he had managed to duplicate and was hoping to get a pat on the back for his quick thinking.

Johnston had managed to push everything aside on his hectic calendar and had even found a suitable candidate to deputize for him and delegate all his duties as head of the British Museum-sponsored winter archaeological dig. This cover-up operation would make him less conspicuous and enable him to devote his full attention to keeping track of Drake and ensuring both he and his band of reprobates were always one step ahead.

When Beaver arrived back at Selim's safe house in Luxor, Johnston was already there enjoying a smooth eighteen-year-old Glenlivet malt whiskey, breathing in the subtle aromas of the golden liquor and relishing the Speyside dram aged in a combination of American oak and sherry casks.

"This is a fine single malt, Selim, and I suspect difficult to come by over here, so a welcome treat." Then, addressing Beaver in a more aggressive tone, Johnston squawked, "Well then! Hand over the photographs so we can take a good look at them!"

Beaver pushed the envelope across the wooden table. Johnston put down his Waterford-Crystal tumbler and snapped up the envelope and spread out the stack of enlarged prints.

"Good work, Beaver! This will certainly put us on an even keel for now, and I'll undoubtedly need to channel all my wits to get the text translated as quickly as possible to keep ahead of the game! However, notwithstanding this, even if Drake does manage to outmaneuver us on the last hurdle and unravel the script before us, all will not be lost. We can just use them to lead us to wherever the trail ends, and you two can get rid of them both once and for all."

"Thanks, boss. That sounds good to me, as I really had to hold myself back from giving him one at the hotel in Aswan!" Beaver remarked.

"That's the difference between you and I, you have to think smart, or you'll always be a loser. I'm glad we have you on a tight leash for now, as I don't want any more cockups similar to what happened on your Red Sea jaunt, as we have too much at stake here!"

Beaver clenched his fists as his cheeks began to flush with anger. He didn't particularly like Johnston's rebuff after what had seemed to be a positive turn of events, and with much effort he managed to control his temper and decided this would be a good opportunity to leave the room and get out of Johnston's hair.

"Okay, no need to keep bringing up that shit, and don't forget, I wasn't alone there, so you can't pin it all on me. I'll see this through, and once we finish the job, you can pay me my dues, and I'll be out of your life once and for all. I'll leave you alone and wait for further instructions in due course. Good evening to you." He left Selim's office.

"Keep a close handle on that one, as I still don't trust his abilities, particularly over here."

"Absolutely, Mr. Johnston! You can count on me, and if I have any cause for concern, I'll just get rid of him too!" Selim chuckled.

Johnston helped himself to another dram of whiskey and picked up one of the photographs, which spoke to him right away, as he could see the author telling a story about the king. Why had this been hidden? Wanting to get back to his hotel suite and have access to his personal reference library, which he always had ready for just such inscriptions, he bade farewell to Selim and had a driver take him back to the Hilton.

Once in his palatial suite, he studied the photographs intently, and like Sherry he scribbled down notations on a lined yellow legal pad that he had brought with him from his office in London.

CHAPTER 20

The interpretation of the scrolls was proving far more elusive than what both investigating parties would have envisaged. The riddles that Siptah had written on the ancient parchment were astonishingly inconclusive, though very intriguing, as it read more like fiction than fact.

Sherry had told George that she didn't want to leave the hotel until they had completed the job, which rested entirely on her shoulders and was becoming more burdensome by the day.

She was always conscious that they were being watched and made sure she kept her working papers by her side at all times. She only moved between their room and a specially reserved table in a quiet area of the restaurant patio, overlooking the Nile. In the distance, she could also see the Valley of the

Kings, which she knew was beckoning them by the day, and she was itching to get out there and start looking for more clues.

Three days had passed since returning from Aswan, and Sherry was getting more frustrated. She briefed George with her latest translation of the intricate hieroglyphics. As they sat back and relaxed in their bamboo Rattan reclining chairs and sipped on a sundowner, Sherry began to recount her annotation of Siptah's tale at a whisper to add to the tension in the air.

"For anyone who finds this note, let it be known that this is my account of all the wrongs that I have done to my Pharaoh Horemosis and that it was I who took his life so early. I was deeply spurned on by my own jealousy for his wife, Hatshepsut, whom I loved so dearly and who I know was not of this earth but a goddess from another world. It was I who found Hatshepsut after she fell from the skies, and it was I who taught her our ways and first showed her to the king, while she was still entombed in her sarcophagus, which had crashed into our sacred mountain in a ball of flame.

"She was beautiful, and her knowledge was far beyond anything our scholars could ever dream to match. She taught us much while she lived with us, and I became very envious when my pharaoh announced that he would take her as his queen. When she became pregnant with his child, my anger became even more incensed, and it was then that I decided to rid myself of the pharaoh. As his high priest, I could rule in his place until the child became of age and do as I so wished. The pregnancy was shorter than what we are accustomed to, and the baby developed quickly. When the baby was about to be born, I drugged Hatshepsut to make it look as if she had died in childbirth and had the babe handed over to a wet nurse. I called Horemosis and showed him the body of Hatshepsut, which had feigned death, and as he leaned over her, I took his dagger and thrust it into his heart and wrapped his hands around the hilt so the guards would think it was an act of suicide.

"In my capacity as high priest, I then undertook all the embalming and burial responsibilities. We had already built his tomb into the mountain at the same place Hatshepsut had arrived from the skies. I embalmed our king, and in place of Hatshepsut, I embalmed another girl of the same age so as to avoid discovery. The night of our king's death, I took

Hatshepsut back to her own sarcophagus and placed her next to the dead man she had arrived with, then sealed her in just as it was many moons previous on that night she came from the stars. I then sealed the room with bricks and had the walls painted and inscribed to hide her from all for eternity. After Horemosis was buried with all glory, I killed all those who knew the location of this tomb, and only those who possess these scrolls will ever know the fate of Horemosis and his queen and the whereabouts of his tomb, which can be found in his blood on this papyrus."

"Well," George remarked, "that's one hell of a story and beautifully told. What are your thoughts as a budding Egyptologist, and does this make any sense to you?"

"It's clearly a sort-of confession and something he never wanted anyone else to find out. You know our scholars always documented the history of our kings, and clearly Siptah wanted to maintain this tradition but at the same time keep it hidden. He only wanted any discovery of his wrongdoing to happen way after his death. As a high priest, the events must have been extremely important bearing in mind he makes reference to the queen coming to earth from beyond the stars. One other thing that's quite obvious is that we need to take another close look at the original scrolls, but this time under UV light. You'll recall he made reference to the fact that the location of the tomb was somehow inscribed on the document in the blood of the pharaoh. If there's still evidence of any blood, then maybe UV light will show this? If not, I think we could be here for years and still never find anything."

"Agreed," George said and sighed. "I suspect the antiquities department may have access to other more sophisticated equipment that could analyze the document further; however, I don't want to go down that route, at least for now. Let me go and see if I can find a UV source in one of the stores nearby, and I'll meet you back in the room in an hour."

"Sounds like a good idea to me. I'll hang around here for a few more minutes, then head back. Try and be as fast as you can, and remember to keep an eye out for anyone following you."

George slipped out trying to keep a low profile and jumped into a cab near the entrance. He asked the driver to take him to an electronics store and wait for him outside. The drive took ten minutes, and there was plenty of space in front of the shop for the driver to park and wait.

Once in the shop, George had trouble finding what he was looking for.

"Sir, we no have ultra-violet torch, but we do have a UV bulb which maybe will be helpful instead?"

"Okay, that may do the trick, I'll take it."

George paid the shopkeeper, took the bulb, and headed back to the hotel. Once they reached the turning point to the hotel, George asked the driver to stop so he could walk the rest of the way as a security precaution. Once back in the room, he showed Sherry the UV bulb.

"Unfortunately, they didn't have any torches; however, this may work better, as it will be a lot stronger, and we can douse all the lights and just use the UV in one of our lamps instead."

"Good thinking, George! Let's do this now. I can't bear waiting any longer. The suspense is killing me."

George took one of their bedside lights, removed the shade, and inserted the UV bulb and switched it on. The blue light resonated and already had an effect of highlighting any white or fluorescent material that made UV a popular special effect for discos and dance halls.

"Get the scrolls, and let's take a look at them under the lamp," George instructed.

Sherry opened up the safe and took out the folder and carefully extracted the three brittle sheets of papyrus. Closing the curtains and switching off all other lighting, she then gently held each scroll under the light to see if it revealed any other hidden secrets.

"Dammit, I can't see anything," Sherry said.

While disappointed, George suggested turning them over and thoroughly examining the rear of each document.

The first two sheets still revealed nothing of interest; however, the third parchment behaved as they had hoped, and an outline began to materialize of a diagram along with some additional script.

"Wow! Quickly make a copy of this on your pad, and note down everything you see, as we certainly can't do this every time we want to check it out, and also we don't want to risk the message disappearing for any reason," George said.

Sherry sketched out the diagram as best she could and scribbled down the final part of Siptah's confession. She read it aloud to George.

"In my Pharaoh's own blood I write my final note of confession that on this very day I laid him to rest in a sacred spot in a valley to the far west of our sacred mountain well away from the area we have designated for the burial of our future kings. March down this valley from the first set of rocks on your right to a point three thousand five hundred and thirty-three cubits. On the left you will see many rocks that have fallen away from the mountain. One rock, shaped like a serpent, marks the foot of where the tomb starts below the ground and where the bodies of the guards and builders of these tunnels now rest. I am sorry for what I have done, my king, and will live the rest of my life in regret for my actions. May you live forever in happiness in the heavens. Signed Siptah High Priest of Thebes."

"This is it, and just what we've been waiting for!" exclaimed George.

"Tomorrow morning I'll go into town and gather a few additional supplies, then let's head to the other side of the river and start looking for this intriguing valley. We can use a GPS to measure the precise distance and 3,533 cubits should equate to around 1,615 meters at the rate of 1 cubit to 0.46 meters."

George replaced the original bulb back into the bedside light, then locked up their precious scrolls back into the safe and started thinking about what minimal equipment they should procure to uncover the entrance to the tomb.

"You know, Sherry, bearing in mind we know roughly where the entrance is, we could, if we're lucky, unearth it fairly quickly using the tools now available to us. Most of what we need we can probably get from a plant-hire company. Do you know anyone trustworthy who can supply us with a few items?"

"Let me make a few calls to Cairo, as we have some friends who are pretty big contractors, and they for sure will be able to point us in the right direction."

Not wanting to use their room telephone for fear of being overheard, they decided to turn in for the night and do everything from town where they would have less likelihood of being bugged.

CHAPTER 21

It was yet another restless night, and both George and Sherry got very little sleep. In the morning, they were keen to skip breakfast and at last leave the confines of the hotel and follow Siptah's final clue to what they hoped would be the pharaoh's definitive resting place.

Stopping at a coffee shop to grab a quick croissant and cappuccino, Sherry asked if she could make a call to her office in Cairo but instead dialed her uncle who she had mentioned was in the construction trade.

"Hi Uncle, I know this is a very strange request, but I'm in Luxor at the moment and wondered if you know of any plant-hire companies here that may be willing to lease out some tools that I need for a few days."

"Sherifa, of course. I'm always keen to help the antiquities department." After a couple minutes he came back with a suggested contact. "Stop by the branch of Egypt Tool Hire Company located on Al Qarna Street near the Luxor stables, and ask for Mohammed. I'll give him a call now and tell him to expect you and that I will take care of the bill as better to have it billed through my construction company."

"Oh, thank you so much! That would be great, and I'll make it up to you somehow."

"Don't you worry, Sherifa, you're like my own daughter, and what I would do for her I would do for you too. When you're back in Cairo, do give me a call, and come over and see us, as it's been far too long!"

"Thank you again, baba. I will, and I'm really looking forward to it."

Sherry hung up by which time George had already paid for and collected their coffees and pastries. While sipping down the piping-hot drinks out of flimsy paper cups, Sherry announced the great news. George then gave a quick rundown of his thoughts on the subject.

"Since we'll be in stealth mode, and it's only going to be the two of us, we really should limit ourselves to what we can carry with us in the Jeep, as I reckon we can probably drive right up to the spot and tuck ourselves away behind a rocky crag while we check out the site. As it happens, I've already been giving some thought to what we should take and think we can get away with just a few basic items, like a portable ground-penetrating-radar device. GPR is widely used now by archeologists to map subsurface strata and will enable us to quickly scan for tunnels and voids in the same way it's used by contractors to avoid digging up pipes.

"If we locate an area of interest, we'll need a backpack core drill, and I suspect around ten meters of twenty-six millimeter sectional drill pipe, ideal for accessing difficult areas. If we manage to drill into a void, we can use something like a Viper mini-core inspection camera, which comes in a compact case and will provide immediate high-definition images of whatever is at the other end of the borehole. It has built-in halogen lighting, so we should get some good pictures, and maybe it will help us access where we can probe for a physical entrance to the tunnel. It should also have at least fifty meters of cable for us to play with.

"In addition to these key items, I'll also need the usual pickaxe and shovel and mustn't forget a handheld GPS monitor for gauging the precise distance we'll need to travel from the entrance point of the valley to where X marks the spot. One other thing we need to remember is to carry a couple of jerricans of potable water, for lubricating the drill bit and keeping us hydrated while we're out there. Before we leave here, let's also stock up with some sandwiches, health bars, and some fruit, as I have a feeling we may need to work through the night, so we should prepare for at least a two- to three-day jamboree."

"You really have planned everything for us well ahead of time, and all this sounds great. I must say if we were back in the days of Howard Carter, none of this would be possible without a team of laborers to do all the legwork. I can't wait to get out there!" Sherry chuffed.

After stocking up with additional provisions, including a few extra bottles of Siwa mineral water, which would be useful later for refilling from the larger water cans, they headed back to the Jeep and drove out of town crossing the Nile via the Luxor Bridge.

Once on the west bank, they drove past many of the ancient-Theban necropolises and mortuary temples, including that of Hatshepsut, all of which were located at the base of the rugged hills that were home to the Valley of the Kings and queens and also their target valley where they expected to find the tomb of Horemosis.

It was relatively painless to find the Egypt Tool Hire Company as Al Qarna Street was the main road passing through the western part of Luxor, and having driven past the stables, which were also easily recognizable, they spotted the company's bright neon sign and maneuvered the Jeep into the adjacent yard area.

Sherifa took over control and asked for Mohammed who was already expecting them.

As the requested items were all typically in stock, they had no difficulty in acquiring everything that George had requested, all of which fit nicely in the back of the Jeep having made additional room by putting down the back seats.

The onward drive to the main parking area of the Valley of the Kings only took another ten minutes. It was full of taxis and buses, and there was a host of tourists walking back and forth enjoying the spectacular sights of the tombs that were open to the public.

Turning a hard right just past the parking area, they were able to make their way without being questioned by any security personnel and drove past the tomb of Rameses VII (KV1), which was located right at the entrance area to the tombs. Instead of driving into what was known as the West Valley, which was adjacent to the Valley of the Kings, they forked right again up a narrow desert path into anther more desolate valley, which up to now had remained untouched and of no further interest, bearing in mind practically all the kings and queens of the Eighteenth to Twentieth Dynastic periods had already been discovered.

"Switch on the GPS distance monitor so we can mark on the map where we are, as the first outcrop of rocks will start just about here. I'll also use the vehicle odometer as a backup."

Sherry stepped out of the Jeep and lined up the gadget, which sported a large LCD display with the rocky outcrop. She then zeroed the counter and pressed the button to start measuring. Once back in the car, George pulled the lever to put the car into four-wheel-drive low, as it looked like there was quite of lot of loose sand on the unblemished valley floor.

Keeping her eye on the monitor, Sherry shouted out the yardage every hundred meters, and when they had finally meandered the vehicle up the track and reached 1,500 meters, George slowed the vehicle to a crawl, and with increasing excitement Sherry counted up every ten meters reducing to every meter after 1,600 until they hit their final goal of 1,615 meters.

George double-checked the odometer and deduced they were within a tenth of a kilometer of the target area, which was the best outcome he could have hoped for from the less accurate of the two devices. He then parked the vehicle as close to the rocks as possible in an effort to conceal it from the pathway and switched off the engine.

"Bring over the distance tracker so we can mark off the starting point of our search area, as I suspect allowing for measuring anomalies, it could be anywhere within a radius of fifty to a hundred meters from our X-marks-the-spot waypoint. The transcript had mentioned we should look for a serpent-shaped rock on the left-hand side, but I'm not sure after some three and half thousand years, whether we'll have much chance of locating this, as the erosion and subsequent landfalls may have removed all evidence of it."

Sherry handed the GPS monitor to George who then took out a piece of white chalk and marked an X on a piece of rock at the base of the valley wall.

Having also stocked up with a ball of green garden twine and some pegs, he then proceeded to mark off two straight lines fifty meters apart on either side of the marker and running a distance of about five meters each ninety degrees out from the rock face. Once the large rectangular search area was marked off, he then assembled the GPR machine and rolled it over to the right-hand outer corner of the prospect zone and explained how he was going to survey the complete grid.

"I'm going to run this machine up and down the pegged-out area of interest, like a lawn mower. The machine has a built-in computer and display screen and will interpret what lies beneath the surface. The base of the unit, which houses the antenna, sends out tiny pulses of energy into the ground fed by the control panel, which it transmits and then amplifies. These signals are reflected back and picked up by the unit for us to then interpret. The key to establishing if there's any void or tunnel will depend on the strength and time these signals take to get back, which are recorded by the computer and illustrated on the display panel. I haven't actually used one of these before; however, from what I've been told we should be able to spot voids very easily, as there will be a definitive gap shown on the display if we run over one, otherwise the reflected signals will appear consistent and unremarkable. If gaps do show up in the same spot on other parallel runs, then we've likely found ourselves a possible tunnel and should mark each anomaly with a little flag so we can check them out later. I've been told to set the primary antenna at two hundred megahertz, which will be good for depths from zero to nine meters."

Having switched on the machine's power, George started to push the gadget in a crisscross formation slowly and methodically looking for any deviations in the signals that were now being displayed on the computer screen.

Unbeknownst to Drake, at the crest of one of the jagged peaks overlooking the desolate valley, Beaver was peering at him through a pair of high-powered Steiner HX 15x56 binoculars.

Johnston had already given up two days trying to get any sense from the photographs, as he knew a vital piece of information was missing on the recorded images, which would make it impossible for him to discover the whereabouts of the missing tomb and that he would have to rely on Drake and the girl to do all the hard work and take over once they found it.

Selim had had one of his men fit a tracking device to Drake's Jeep while they were still at their hotel and had been able to follow their every move.

Having been instructed to call in Drake's movements, Beaver decided to update Johnston.

"Good afternoon, Mr. Johnston, I'm pleased to report that I have both Drake and the girl in sight. From what I can see, it looks like they may be onto something, as they've already marked off an area they appear to be surveying. How do you want me to play this out?"

"Stay put for now, and just continue to watch them. We don't want to move in too quickly. Only when it looks like they've struck gold will we make our move, do you understand!? I have Selim and a gang of his men on standby, and when the time comes, we'll join Mr. Drake and the girl and seal their fate."

CHAPTER 22

The GPR survey proceeded just as Drake had hoped, and within two meters of the rock face, not far from the original marker, he picked up the differing signal he was looking for. Marking it off and turning around he picked it up again and again as he got closer to the valley wall. The signals also clearly showed that the tunnel's starting point was only about a meter from the surface and that the closer he got to the rock face, the deeper it went measuring about two meters wide.

"Sherry! I think I've found something. I'm going to use the core drill now to see if we've located our tomb entry point and the even better news is that we won't have to drill very far!"

Leaving the GPR machine by the Jeep, George opened the back and reached for the backpack containing the core drilling unit and also grabbed a couple extra pipe extensions just in case he needed to drill down a bit further. The diamond drill bit could cut through about a meter of rock with one section of pipe before needing an extension unit coupled to the main drill pipe.

"Can you fetch the case with the core inspection unit? I think I could cut through this fairly quickly," George said.

"Sure thing. I can't wait to get a close look at what's down there."

George fired up the two-stroke engine, breathing in some of the inevitable black smoke that billowed out of the exhaust manifold, and made sure the diamond-studded drill bit was properly secure and that the water-supply hose was adequately fed by one their water cans to lubricate the bit as it drilled through the rock.

Gripping the double-handled, twenty-kilo device and holding it steady between his legs, he depressed the start button and kicked the drill into action boring out a twenty-six-millimeter wide hole, which would deliver a twenty-millimeter core sample.

The supposed limestone rock foundation was not as hard as they had anticipated, and within ten minutes he was already onto his second rod. Five minutes into that, he felt the bit suddenly sink and knew right away he was all the way through. Removing the rod and inspecting the core sample retrieved from the two encased steel sections, they could see that the physical strata of the drill site was not that solid and that the void space below was mainly covered by a granite slab (probably specially commissioned for sealing the tomb) measuring approximately twelve inches thick. Placed on top of that was a mixture of compressed sand and rock fill that would ultimately hide the whereabouts of the pharaoh for eternity.

The Viper mini-pipe-inspection camera fitted nicely in the borehole. It had a six-millimeter camera head surrounded by four integral high-output LED lights. George connected the camera head to a twenty-meter, PVC-coated, fiberglass insertion probe that was connected to the main lightweight carrying case that housed a TV monitor and built-in mini-cassette recorder to record the images they were about to see.

"This is the moment of truth," George said feeling a little apprehensive.

"Go for it. I can't wait any longer! The suspense is excruciating!" Sherry squealed.

Switching on the camera, the high-powered lights were almost blinding, but the narrow beam quickly diminished as he inserted the unit down into the drilled orifice and fed the cable pushing the camera end deep into the dark abyss.

Once down in the void, George was able, using one of the controls on the panel board, to alter the angle of the camera to get a clearer, 360-degree view. What became apparent were the vast number of skeletons and bones lying loosely at the base of the granite slab and which stretched for some distance along the tunnel confines deeper into the mountainside. These would have all been from the bodies of workers and guards who knew of the tomb's whereabouts and who would have been killed at the time of sealing the tomb.

It was not possible to see much else or even where the sealed entrance was, as this would have been considerably further down the tunnel. Nevertheless there was enough evidence for George to dig down, expose the slab, and make a hole large enough for them to crawl into and explore the area before deciding what they should do next in terms of notifying the respective authorities and claiming the discovery rights.

"Can you get me a bottle of water from the back of the Jeep and maybe one of those sandwiches we picked up from the cafe this morning?" George asked as he started to remove his shirt in preparation for some back-breaking navy work.

Sherry returned with a bottle of Siwa and a cheese-and-salad sandwich, which George quickly scarfed down. He then grabbed the pickaxe and started to break up the sandy ground around the drilled borehole.

"Oh, I like those chiseled muscles. God, you're super fit, *habibi*! I reckon you'll be ready for a nice rubdown after we finish here and announce the find of the century!" Sherry teased.

"Talk about digging graves. We have about six feet of rubble to excavate here, and what I intend to do, since the ground seems pretty firm, is dig down in a step formation to make getting in and out much easier once we reach the granite block."

By now the sun was beginning to hide behind the west side of the mountain range, and George sighed with relief as the outside temperature began to cool and an evening breeze picked up tempo and blew down the desolate valley.

After a couple hours of alternating between the pickaxe and shovel, George finally felt a thud as he hit the pink-granite slab.

"We need to be careful here not to crack the whole slab, as I may end up collapsing it and injuring myself. To make life easier, I'm going to take the core-drilling machine and drill a number of holes to make a circle about two feet in diameter. After this, I'll give it a few whacks with the pickaxe, and with a bit of luck, it should break and drop to the bottom of the pit."

The sky was almost pitch black, and the only lights that could be seen were the bright reflections cast by an almost full moon and the billions of dazzling stars, which due to the clean air provided a beautiful and romantic backdrop.

Fortunately, they both still had their powerful dive flashlights, as well as a small backup, self-powered dynamo that would give them enough light in the tomb.

Walking up the steps he had just carved out from the hardened surface, George made his way to the back of the Jeep and briefed Sherry about what they might need to access the tomb.

"I'm going to take the drill with us, as well as the pickaxe and spade and one of the jerricans of water for us as and for lubricating the drill bit. We'll need to carry all our torches, and I suspect we should probably try and keep ourselves a bit warmer and maybe take our neoprene wet-suit tops, as these could also give us a little extra body protection. Let's use our dive bag in the back of the car and stuff all the smaller items into it. In the meantime, I'm going to start drilling all the holes to forge out an access point."

Sherry heard George start drilling out the hardened granite slab and took over putting together the balance of the supplies. Included in the dive bag were the rest of their food supplies and a few extra bottles of water. She also took their camera and a few extra rolls of film, knowing full well they would need to visually document their find. She then locked up the Jeep and made her way back to the quarried trench, dive bag in hand.

As the granite was only about twelve inches thick, the powerful core drill's diamond bit cut through it very easily, and each hole only took about a minute to glide through from one end to the other. George rapidly drilled out twenty twenty-six millimeter holes and concluded this would be enough to weaken the granite block and enable him to finish the job with his pickaxe. With a just few heavy swings of the pick, the central portion gave way and plunged to the bottom of the tunnel's entry point, landing with a thud and splintering all the bones beneath.

"We're through! Torches on, and let's get down there and see what we can find. Hopefully there are no more snakes or creepy-crawlies. You take the bag, and I'll bring down the rest of our gear."

The jump down from the drilled-out section was effortless, as it was only about five feet from the base, and this would also allow for an easy exit.

Their flashlight beams revealed what carnage must have occurred at the time of sealing up the entrance to the tomb as there were remains of hundreds of slain bodies strewn from wall to wall, most of which were contorted evidencing a terrifying demise. After about fifty feet of trudging through stacks of brittle bones, the confined tunnel opened out into a cavernous area, and it was evident that the walls of the cavern had been sculptured out by something other than natural geological conditions, like an external force or explosion. The resultant super-heat damage had created a glass-like residue that looked almost like a shiny wallpaper had been pasted from floor to ceiling. The ground must have also been cleared of all the rubble and fallout and neatly filled in to make way for the pharaoh's final resting place.

At the end of the scorched cave was the tomb entrance with two gigantic wooden doors almost twenty feet in height and width and sealed with the cartouche of Horemosis.

"This is unbelievable!" exclaimed Sherry. "Of all the tombs discovered to date, there has been nothing like this. The size of everything is mind-blowing. He must have been a great king and the true founder of the dynastic rulers who followed."

"Will anything happen if and when we break the seal?" George inquired with a slight shiver. The temperature in the cavern was already quite chilly and triggered goosebumps, not to mention he was also thinking about the supposed pharaoh's curse that was linked to the Carnarvons at the time of Howard Carter's discovery of Tutankhamun in KV62.

"Nonsense, there was no such thing as the pharaoh's curse, and all the events experienced by Lord Carnarvon and even his own death were entirely coincidental. They were merely rumors to put off foreigners from discovering new findings so that the desert dwellers and tomb keepers could be the beneficiaries of any such revelations," Sherry said.

Cutting the seal with one of their dive knives, George then inserted the blade in the crevice between the two enormous ebony doors, which must have been imported from Africa and could only be afforded by the extremely wealthy.

After over 3,500 years of being closed, the doors inched open enough for George and Sherry to pass through.

Stashing the dive bag and bulk of their other equipment to one side behind some large alabaster urns at the entrance to the enormous antechamber, they began to explore the tomb.

The walls of the voluminous hall were decorated with thousands of exquisite and colorful paintings depicting much of the pharaoh's life and exploits during his era. Other large alabaster urns were also neatly placed around the room adding to the regal touch and further demonstrating his importance as a great ruler.

Another archway to the right of the main hallway led them to yet another anteroom, this time filled with many of what would have been the pharaoh's finest personal belongings. These stately possessions would have provided him with everything he would have needed in life after death, and for eternity thereafter. They found gilded furniture, weapons, jewelry, and even chariots very similar to what Howard Carter would have seen when he first ventured into Tutankhamun's burial chambers, but on a much grander scale.

In the next slightly smaller room, they found the eight traditional, ornate alabaster jars sealed with tops shaped with the face of Anubis, containing the internal organs of both the pharaoh and what they assumed would belong to his queen. Other personal items were stacked up against the painted walls, and at the far end of the room was the final archway leading to the inner burial chamber and two majestic, pink-granite sarcophagi emblazoned with carved hieroglyphics again depicting the lives of the two embalmed monarchs.

"George, I'm going to head back to the entrance hall to get the camera and extra film, as I think we should make a record of this and not move anything until we've informed the antiquities department and gotten their blessing to lead the logging and retrieval of everything here, not to mention opening up the sarcophagi and taking the first look at the mummies," Sherry said as she backtracked to the entrance where she had left the dive bag.

George watched the beam of her flashlight slowly fade as she navigated her way through the three chambers back to the main hallway. George resumed viewing all the breathtaking and priceless antiquities that now captivated his attention.

CHAPTER 23

Johnston pulled up to the rendezvous point in an official antiquities department-marked Toyota Land Cruiser. The vehicle had been assigned to him for the duration of his stay in Luxor and would ensure freedom of movement within the area and thereby avoid any unnecessary interaction with security guards, if they happened to be wandering around. Selim joined him in another similar Land Cruiser with three additional armed sidekicks.

Beaver, who had called Johnston once George and Sherry had made their entrance, was already waiting for them. He climbed into the passenger seat of Johnston's vehicle, and once they started moving, directed Johnston further up the valley until they were about a hundred yards from Drake's Jeep Wrangler, at which point they turned off their engines and all the lights.

"Selim, you and your boys stick behind us, and try not to fire off any rounds in the tomb, as we don't want to damage anything. Use minimal force only," Johnston commanded.

Selim and his Egyptian heavies all packed a Helwan 920 semiautomatic service revolver, manufactured locally for the Egyptian military and modelled on the Beretta M92-FS pistol. Each of the handguns carried ten rounds of 9x19mm parabellum cartridges in their grip-mounted magazines, originally designed and introduced to the German Army by Georg Luger back in 1902 and still rank as the world's most popular bullets.

Mustering at the base of Drake's neatly dug-out hole, Johnston saw no sign of his quarry and assumed they were somewhere deep inside the tomb. Clambering down from the drilled-out piece of granite, he was in awe of what Drake and the girl had so skillfully located and annoyed that they had found it before him.

With all six of them now present and accounted for inside the cramped entry point, he whispered out further instructions, then led all his crew in single file through the narrow bone-littered tunnel into the spacious cavern.

Within the dark contrast of black abyss that they were now navigating across, Johnston noticed a narrow beam of light that wavered close to the massive, ancient wooden doors that had secured the main entrance to the tomb at the far end of the subterranean grotto. He had noted that the black timber portal was only slightly ajar and as such had shielded their own flashlights from whoever was on the other side.

"Shush, everyone, and switch off your torches. Someone's heading this way."

Sherry was totally unaware that Johnston was approaching on the other side of and continued making her way across the central hallway. As soon as she had passed the gigantic doorway, Johnston motioned to Beaver to grab her.

Ushering one of Selim's men to follow, Beaver crept up behind the crevice between the two doors. While her back was turned, he made a quick dash, throwing himself at the girl and covering her mouth with his large callous-ridden hand. They tumbled to the ground, and with the weight of Beaver's bulky frame on top of her, she found it nearly impossible to breathe and choked, as the fall, coupled with his weight, had knocked the wind out of her.

Beaver rolled her over so she could see the muzzle of the revolver now being pointed at her by the accompanying stooge and motioned her to remain silent.

Johnston and his remaining party members appeared, and Sherry knew they were trapped.

"Beaver, tie her hands behind her back, and gag her, then bring her along with us to the other rooms so we can fish out and secure Drake," Johnston ordered.

Beaver bound Sherry's hands using a small length of rope that they had brought along with them and gagged her with some duct tape. They then proceeded to push her in front of them as they made their way from room to room until they reached the burial chamber where George was still looking around.

"Well, Mr. Drake, we meet once again. I must thank you for doing all the hard work and locating this most exceptional tomb."

Observing Sherry tied up with a gun at her back and that petrified look, he knew there was nothing he could do other than surrender himself and submit to their wants.

"Okay, Johnston, it looks like you've outsmarted us this time, and clearly we have no option other than to hand over our discovery. Go ahead, take credit for it. I just hope you'll consider letting us both go quietly." George tested the waters.

"Oh no, no, no! You have me all wrong. I have no interest in taking credit for any discovery. Far from it! We want to keep this place well away from prying eyes, at least until we've managed to extract many of these wonderful artefacts from here, without our friends at the antiquities department knowing about it. These treasures will most certainly fetch more than a pretty penny on the black market and lead me to what I think will be an extremely well earned early retirement. Selim, along with his colleagues in Cairo, will provide us with all the resources we need to execute the operation discretely."

"If that's the case, then what do you propose to do with us?" George inquired feeling nervous that their fate might be hanging by a very thin thread, as they almost certainly wouldn't want them alive and in a position to rat out the devious nature of their plan. Considering what they had already experienced in Sharm El-Sheikh and their lucky escape from the *Thistlegorm* event, these guys had no scruples in eliminating anyone who stood in their way.

Beaver laughed while pulling the gag from Sherry's mouth.

"You'd better tie up young Mr. Drake here, and I suggest you tie their legs as well," Johnston ordered. "We'll need to get out of here before light and remove all the vehicles to keep this area cordoned off as best we can and also camouflage the excavated trench."

Turning toward Selim he said, "Make sure we have someone posted on the hills at all times to keep anyone hiking up this valley well clear of the spot. As for now, I think we can take a few smaller items with us and come back tomorrow evening with a truck and additional labor to remove some of the larger pieces and have similar runs every other night until we think the time has come to spill the beans and announce the find to the antiquities department and conclude that the tomb had long ago been a victim of tomb robbers, like so many others"

"That sounds too easy to me, but you still haven't answered my question," George said.

"All in good time, Drake, just tell me where your car keys are, as you won't be needing them anymore."

Sherry's eyes welled up with tears. "I have the keys in my pocket," she murmured.

"Beaver, take their keys, and when we leave here, you drive the Jeep back to Selim's yard, and keep it out of sight. We may be able to use it later to dispose of them if we need to. I'm going to show you what items we can take with us tonight. I want to move out soon before we become too noticeable!"

Johnston proceeded to point out a number of exquisitely crafted pieces of jewelry along with a few of the smaller characteristic statues, portraying both the pharaoh and various deities of the period. He also found a sensational jewel-encrusted golden dagger and instructed Selim's men to carry all the selected objects back to his Land Cruiser.

On their return the next evening, he would make sure that he had enough men to open up the two sarcophagi and remove any valuable items from within and leave the mummies in situ for the antiquities department to relish as a great discovery. Having made some additional rough notes of what else they could remove upon their return visit the following night, he concluded that they would need to try and complete the whole removal process within two or three days and then adjust the opening as if it had been plundered by others long ago and announce the complete discovery of the tomb to be numbered KV66 under the guise of his role as archaeological-dig leader for the British Museum-sponsored winter excavation.

Returning back to Drake, he said, "To answer your earlier question, I have no wish to kill you both. Instead we're going to leave you to stew here so you can enjoy the tomb in complete darkness until I decide what to do with you. There will be no escape, as we're going to leave you tied up and close off the tomb until we return, at which point, if you're still alive, we'll leave it up to Selim to take care of you. On that note, I bid you farewell! Sleep tight, Mr. Drake."

Johnston left the room with the rest of his gang of ruffians, and as they departed, the light began to diminish, and the room became darker and darker, until it faded into blackness.

Sherry was now inconsolable and burst into tears. Clutching as best she could from her bound-up position she rested her head on George's shoulder thinking this would be the end of them and that they should not have attempted to solve the mystery single-handedly.

George, with an encouraging resonance, lifted her spirits.

"Don't worry, my darling, I think I may be able to at least free us from these binds."

"How are you going to manage that?"

"Well, because Johnston and his gang of gorillas were so engrossed with the spoils, they must have assumed we were unarmed and didn't search us before tying us up. I still have the dive knife strapped to my leg underneath my trousers, so if you can somehow reach that, we may be able to cut the rope and free each other. I also have my reserve self-powered torch with me, so we should be able to get back to our bag stashed near the entrance and see what might be left. Now, you wriggle on the floor, and see if you can grab the knife from my leg."

Sherry was charged with a new burst of energy and lay down on the dust-covered floor with her head facing George's feet. She then rolled back and forth while inching herself nearer and nearer and adopting a sort of caterpillar motion until her hands, which were still tied behind her back, could feel the bottom of George's right tibia and the welcome bulge of his dive knife, neatly hidden beneath his worn denim jeans and secured by a snug Teflon leg-strap sheath.

"That's it, Sherry, now try to pull up my trouser leg, and use your fingers to grasp the blade. It has an easy handle, as you can slot your fingers in the five holes, which should give you a firm grip, especially in our current position, and you'll need to make sure you hold it tight with the knife facing up. The blade has a really sharp serrated edge, so if I can work the point through any part of my bindings and shift my weight a bit, we can probably cut through this rope."

After some uncomfortable maneuvering, Sherry finally got her right-hand fingers and thumb slotted into the five holes drilled through the blackened stainless-steel grip and managed to turn onto her side with the blade facing up toward her neck.

"I won't be able to sit up, so you'll have to try and work it through on your side like me."

"Okay, that should work too, but make sure you keep a tight hold of the grip, as this will probably be our only chance. Stay as you are, and I'll get my hands close to the blade and let you know when I'm ready."

Every minute that passed seemed more like an hour, and this was certainly not as straightforward as George had hoped. However, luck and determination prevailed, and after a few more tense moments, he at last managed to get the knife's serrated edge in between one of the bonds."

"Stand by, honey! I'm going to start working the blade into the rope."

Sherry gripped tightly on the hilt with all her might, knowing full well that if she let go that could be the end of them. Using all his bodyweight and lying on the floor behind her, George manipulated the razor-sharp blade between his bindings and in a gentle up-and-down motion sawed through the rope's ligatures. Almost instantly, rope strands began to fray and pull apart as he worked against the knife. Soon he felt the rope give way, and as he pushed his arms outward, the cord finally broke and both arms shot out with the sudden release of tension.

"*Al hamdullilah!*" screamed George adopting the popular Arabic phrase "Praise be to God" or more commonly "Thank God!" George continued, "I'll take the knife now and cut all the remaining bindings, and we can then check see what Johnston left us, as I doubt he'll have seen the dive bag as it would have been out of sight behind those jars."

George proceeded to cut through the remaining rope that was tied around his legs and thereafter attended to Sherry and released her from her shackles, which by now had already begun to cut into the soft flesh around her wrists. Digging into his pocket, George pulled out his self-powered dynamo flashlight and quickly turned the crank handle to fire up the bulb. While not as powerful as their dive flashlights, it gave enough light to be able to move around the tomb and find their way back to the main hallway.

"It looks like when they grabbed you, your torch must have switched itself off as it hit the ground, and as a result, they overlooked picking it up. If you can grab it and turn it on, I can put this one away for later in case we need it again."

Sherry was grateful to see that her flashlight still worked as she turned on the powerful Dive Rite EX35 Primary Canister Light. "I'm surprised no one picked this up, as Sunny told me that it retails around $1,300, and good thing for us it has a twenty-four-hour battery, so if we use it on quarter power it will still deliver us plenty of light at around a thousand lumens."

"Lucky for us! Let's have a drink and something to eat as I'm sure you're parched, and I suspect we have about twenty hours before Johnston returns," George said.

Opening up the dive bag, George handed Sherry one of the remaining bottles of Siwa water and split the last of their cheese sandwiches with her.

"What are we going to do for a restroom here? I'm near bursting," Sherry said.

"That's a good point. I really need to relieve myself as well, even though I'm a bit dehydrated from all the hard work yesterday! I think we should use one of the urns over there," he said, pointing to one of the large alabaster pots strategically placed around the hallway.

After refreshing themselves, George took a look at the large ebony doors and gave them a push. "I think Johnston must have wedged the doors tight on the other side, so we won't have much luck pushing them from this end, and even though I have the pickaxe, it looks as if they took our drill." George sighed, out of ideas about how to exit the tomb.

"You know, there should still be another room, as according to Siptah's scrolls, he placed Hatshepsut in a separate chamber and sealed her in next to another person who he mentioned had arrived with her from the stars. Why did he do that? And what's in there? I think we should see if we can find her. If you remember, he said he'd had the walls painted after sealing her in, and I suspect the final clue to finding the entry point will be within these paintings, particularly as he seems to have been so infatuated with her."

"I agree," said George. "There's no harm in checking this out, and if we make the hole small enough we can try and cover our tracks and hide in there, and if anyone tries to follow us in we should have more of an upper hand."

Sherry started making her way around the walls of the hallway, as this was the room that had been decorated the most, and at the far end of the enormous chamber almost directly opposite the main entrance she found frescos depicting what must have been a very beautiful woman, dressed as the queen would have been at the time, and one in particular with her arms stretched out reaching for the stars. The entire wall seemed to be dedicated to the queen and depicted her supervising surgical procedures, manufacturing weaponry, and helping her people, almost making her more important than the pharaoh. On top of the centerpiece, and positioned within the stars, was an image of Amun's disk painted in gold with Hatshepsut's cartouche inscribed within it.

"George, Bring the pickaxe over here, and see if you can break through a small hole near the floor so we can crawl through. This should be it if I've interpreted Siptah's mind correctly."

George moved into position and started chipping away at the plaster, careful not to do too much damage to the magnificent artwork. Sherry was spot on, and the wall turned out to be only about a foot thick, separating the two rooms. After carving out a burrow-shaped hole, George pushed the rubble all the way through into the other room and tried to conceal the opening as best he could using one of the large ceramic pots near where he had excavated the opening.

"Grab the dive bag, and let's take it through with us. Also the pickaxe, as we may need to use it to defend ourselves whenever Johnston returns," George suggested. "And if the jerrican's still there, it would be good to have our water supply with us too; we don't know how long we'll have to wait this out."

Sherry made her way back to the entranceway and grabbed their remaining belongings including the water can, then went back to George who was waiting by the hole eager to see what was on the other side. Pushing the bag and water can through the hole first, George then took hold of Sherry's flashlight and slid through the breach, then levied himself upright. Sherry followed, and once her arms were through, George grabbed on to her and pulled her the rest of the way and lifted her to her feet.

The area was even more voluminous than the entry hall they had just left, and it was apparent that the walls and ceiling remained jagged and untouched. Illuminating the area bit by bit with their narrow flashlight beam, the rays suddenly shimmered off a metallic object in the middle of the cavern.

"If this is what I think it is, we may have just discovered the Egyptian equivalent of Area 51," George said, totally awestruck. "This is what Siptah meant when he stated that Hatshepsut had come from the stars and crashed into this very mountainside. You'd have thought the metal would have disintegrated on impact, but it looks as if it's still complete and only mildly tarnished. The material it was built with is probably a lot stronger than anything we have here."

"I can't believe what we've found and what this could bring to the Egyptian people, as this technology would have tremendous value. We can't let Johnston get his hands on this. This is a real-life UFO, and god only knows what's inside," Sherry said, looking for an access point.

There were still remnants of a platform leading to the top of the craft, which Siptah must have used to gain access. By now the wood was pretty brittle but could still take George's weight as he ventured up and sat down on the cool metal zenith and called Sherry to join him.

"The wooden platform still seems okay, and if it can take my poundage you should be more than fine with your sleek frame."

Sherry scrambled up on all fours and jumped next to George. "How do we get inside?"

"There must be some form of pressure switch, as Siptah went to a lot of trouble building this platform, and we know he obviously fathomed it out otherwise he wouldn't have found Hatshepsut. Let's take a closer look around and see if we spot any sort of groove in the metal."

Sherry was by now already brushing her fingers across the cool, almost golden, metallic surface exactly as Horemosis had done when he had first climbed up and stood where they were now. She suddenly called out to George, "I think I can feel something over here," and pointed to an area just below where she was kneeling. As she moved a little further down to get a better look, her knee unexpectedly depressed the well-hidden pressure point, and just as it had opened up in front of the pharaoh, the mechanism worked once again, and the doorway revealed itself with a distinctive buzzing sound. The cold-fusion reactor of the craft was still clearly sufficiently fueled to keep the vessel powered after all these millennia, and as they peered inside, they could see many small lights glowing or flashing on the surrounding control panels.

"This would be the ultimate prize for any nation, as it seems there's almost an unlimited source of energy being generated. If this could be replicated the value would be unfathomable. It would place Egypt at the top of the high table, but at the same time it may be better to keep it hidden as these things can often lead to conflict," George mulled.

"I get your drift, although we're not really in a position to do much right now, and not sure I fancy our chances when Johnston returns," Sherry replied.

"Come, let's take a look around," George exclaimed as he jumped inside landing with a heavy thump onto the metal floor adjacent to what he thought must have been the helm.

"Looks like you won't have to jump after all, as there are some indented grooves where you can slot your feet, which I hadn't noticed from up there."

Sherry followed George's advice and used the hollowed-out notches to make her descent.

Their powerful flashlight, coupled with the lights of the many control panels, encapsulated the area with a bright incandescence. The temperature inside also contrasted with the coldness of the cave. A feeling of warmth radiated through their bodies as they felt the slight hum and vibration of the power plant, which they assumed was housed somewhere deeper within the ship's hull and must have been responsible for maintaining the comfortable environment.

Adjacent to where they stood was a small bannister with more steps leading down another level. They decided to venture below and check out that section.

Once down the stairwell, they identified the two life-support pods, which Horemosis had previously thought were sarcophagi. The metal lids were sealed, and George noted that there were levers integrated into the tops of each container, which he assumed must be some form of safety trigger to allow anyone outside to open or close the units.

Pulling on the lever of the first unit, George felt it give and glide into a secondary locked position, just like an old-fashioned ship's telegraph moving from stop to forward. Once the lever had moved as far as it could and clicked into place, they heard a hiss, then the metal cover enclosing the mechanical cocoon slid back revealing a sealed, glass-covered environment housing the skeletal remains of a humanoid-looking figure that had pretty much disintegrated.

"This really is Area 51, although whoever these aliens were, they're not too different from us. Do you think it could be time travel like in *Planet of the Apes?*" Sherry said.

"Give the second lever a tug and see what happens," George suggested.

Sherry grasped the handle and gave it a yank, and once it too had slid into position, they heard the same characteristic hiss as the lid moved to its open position; however, this time they could not see too much as the glass was heavily frosted, and only a blurred outline of the body lying beneath the sealed panel could be observed.

Unlike what had happened with the first unit, there was some additional automated and machine-like activity on the inside of the tightly sealed chamber. Within seconds a sharp-looking needle-like protrusion moved across from one side of the container and appeared to inject a purple-looking substance into the chest cavity of the body in a seeming state of stasis below the glazed panel. At the same time, the interior took on a glowing-red hue as a number of infrared-looking lights switched on and heated the canister, thawing out all the frosting, and revealing the exquisite beauty of a woman dressed in colorful, pharaonic, linen robes inlaid with lapis, gold, and other colored glass beads. She was perfectly formed and appeared human with light-brown hair that had been cropped short and resembled the queen depicted on the murals.

In her hand, she was still holding onto a stunning golden ankh, which Siptah must have put there before sealing her back into the coffin-like receptacle representing life itself and his desire for Hatshepsut to live forever. Siptah's thoughts when he had sealed the woman's fate three and half thousand years prior were not far off reality.

After a few more minutes staring in wonderment at what they had just uncovered, her fingers began to twitch. The twitching became more erratic as the blood inside her began to circulate more freely, and her vital organs were induced into action. In a flash, her startling, blue-green eyes opened, and as if gasping for air in a state of panic, she reached out for a lever inside her shell and pulled on it prompting the glass panel to move.

George gasped. "She's almost a copy of you, Sherry. This is some form of providence, or maybe you're one of her descendants? Are you able to converse in any ancient-Egyptian dialects of this period? Certainly English will be out of the question."

"I can give it a try, as I've studied the language but have never had an opportunity to have any sort of extensive conversations, other than when I was at the institute studying Egyptology," Sherry responded. Then, turning and facing the woman who was still in a state of shock, she began to slowly speak. "Are you Hatshepsut? You were put to sleep here for a very long time. Thousands of years. We found a message written by a man named Siptah that guided us to you and the tomb of Horemosis who lies nearby."

Tears welled up in Hatshepsut's eyes as she realized what had happened, and her memories returned as if the events from thousands of years prior were only yesterday.

George prompted Sherry to tell her as simply as possible that they were trapped inside the tomb and needed to get out before some bad men with weapons came back and if she had anything that might help them.

Hatshepsut, still very unstable after recovering from her long period of cryogenic inertness, pushed the ankh symbol that she had been holding to one side, sat upright, and tried to pull herself out of the pod. George, feeling for her current state of shock and instability, gently took hold of her left hand, bent down, and placed his head and shoulders next to hers. Putting his other arm around her waist, he then tenderly lifted her out as if also consoling her for all the losses she must have experienced before being shut out of existence. Her skin was soft and delicate, still cool from the ordeal, and as it brushed against George, she felt safe in his arms.

Sherry left to retrieve their dive bag to see if there was anything left that might be useful and also realized Hatshepsut would need to be hydrated. There were also a few health bars left, and they beckoned her to drink and eat to hopefully get some energy back.

Inside the bag, Sherry had also put one of her old T-shirts as well as a pair of shorts in among the neoprene wet suits, which she had packed before their Kom Ombo journey.

After Hatshepsut had taken a few sips of water and eaten one of the snacks, Sherry suggested she change her clothes to blend in with them, as her current dress would raise too many red flags if they were caught.

As she slipped off her colorful linen dress, George couldn't help looking at her striking naked contours, which had a light-milky hue and were totally unblemished. He could not believe she was actually from another world and wondered if our existence on this planet may somehow be linked to her kind, and many questions passed through his mind, which at a more appropriate time he would try to run past her.

Sherry kicked George's foot for staring too much. Moving close to Sherry, he gave her a quick hug as if to say to Hatshepsut that she was his girl and watched Hatshepsut acknowledge the movement with a slight grin on her face signaling that she was becoming more relaxed with her liberators and glad to be back among the living.

Hatshepsut got up and opened a small hatch in the floor, which led down to a small storage locker that had previously never been investigated by Siptah. George followed her down, closely watched by Sherry, and shone his flashlight around the compartment to see what was there. The room was empty, but the circular wall was comprised of drawers and cupboard space that opened automatically when touched.

As she continued to converse with Sherry, she indicated that she had some weaponry that might help them get out and protect themselves if they were attacked.

Opening one of the drawers she pulled out what looked like some form of laser pistol and handed it to George. She then went to one of the other drawers and took out several canisters, which he presumed were a type of explosive device, and handed them over to Sherry to store in their dive bag.

Returning back to the main life-support room, Hatshepsut motioned for them to climb up, take the bag, and exit the ship. She then followed from behind, and after they were all safely out, sealed the hatch. Using the ancient precarious ladder and scaffolding, they climbed back down and headed for their hole in the wall. Having crawled through into the hallway, Sherry showed Hatshepsut the murals depicting her previous life with the pharaoh, and after seeing this, she asked to be taken to Horemosis's sarcophagus so she could at least say a prayer for him.

Time was pressing, and George expected Johnston to return at any time to plunder the tomb once more and probably seal their fate.

Hatshepsut, now more fully aware of their predicament, indicated to Sherry that they must destroy the wall and hide her ship, as she feared what might happen to her if it were to fall into the wrong hands. With this world now far more advanced since her last appearance, it could be extremely dangerous for all of mankind, at least for now, or until she could be absolutely certain that her science and technology would only be used for peaceful purposes and maybe even enable man to explore other worlds for their future benefit.

Taking two of the small canisters out of the bag, she instructed Sherry to place them at strategic locations along the far wall that she carefully pointed out. Once they were in position she went to each one and turned one of the dials and depressed a small trigger button before moving away.

"Quick," she said in her Coptic tongue and motioned to them move to the next room. "I am destroying that wall, and I expect the rock above will cave in," she said to Sherry while making a flurry of additional hand signals.

Safe in the next room, they heard two loud booms and a huge crash as the ceiling along the wall cascaded to the ground, obliterating all evidence of the beautiful painted frescos and leaving an enormous rocky filled barrier between what was left of the hallway and the cave beyond.

George suggested that rather than try and leave the tomb, they would be better off waiting for Johnston and his gang to open the ebony doors and catch them by surprise using the laser weapon that Hatshepsut had recovered from her ship.

The two women agreed and proceeded to look for a suitable vantage point among all the rocks now littering the once-magnificent hallway.

"It's a great pity that we had to destroy this piece of history, and it will probably mean that if we get the tomb cleared by the proper authorities, they'll have to keep it closed, as it will be considered a potentially hazardous area and out of bounds, which should help keep the cave on the other side secret for now," George said leaving Sherry to translate for Hatshepsut.

Sherry then asked her what her actual name was from her people, or whether they should call her by another name, as it would be important to keep her true identity hidden.

"I am called Zolanda by my people," she whispered,

"That's a beautiful name. Is it all right if we shorten it and call you Zoe? Since you two look so similar, we can say that Zoe's your sister," George suggested.

Sherry translated what George had said, and she giggled feeling much more relaxed. She loved his suggestion, as it was so close to what she was normally called, and the idea of having an earthly sister was equally appealing.

While they waited for Johnston to turn up, Sherry started to teach Zoe some English words as she knew that she would be a fast learner having already mastered the ancient-Egyptian language in what must have been a short period of time. She told Zoe their names, which she could now easily repeat, and a few useful words to help them communicate more effortlessly if or when they were in peril. Among her many other amazing talents, Zoe had also been a warrior and was quite used to fighting. Coupled with her more advanced weaponry, she was confident that they would be out of this dark void very soon.

They didn't have to wait long, as very soon after Sherry's English lesson, they heard some loud thuds as Johnston's men hammered the wedges that they had placed under the massive ebony doors the night before.

George shut off the flashlight and handed Zoe the laser weapon, as he was not familiar with how to use it, and Zoe would have been well trained in handling this type of situation.

As the doors opened slightly Selim entered first, followed by Beaver, then Johnston and the three other armed thugs that had tied them up the previous night. They sensed something was not quite right as the atmosphere was still laden with dust and a strong smell from the explosions.

"What the devil happened here?" Johnston roared having noticed that the painted wall at the back of the hall was now a colossal amount rubble.

"It looks like the ceiling collapsed. Maybe we should take what we can and get the hell out of here before the whole roof caves in," Beaver remarked.

"Hmmm, you may have a point, although the rest of the tomb looks pretty well intact. Go and check out Drake and the girl, as we need to get rid of them tonight, and I reckon twenty-four hours of being tied up will have sapped out all their strength. Selim can deal with disposing of their bodies somewhere out in the desert where they'll never be found."

"Aiwa, Mr. Johnston," Selim said.

Beaver headed through the other chambers and made his way to the main burial room where they had tied them up the night before. Reaching the twin sarcophagi he pointed his flashlight at the floor expecting to see the two bodies lying there but instead only saw the cut pieces of rope. "They've gone!" he said.

By now Johnston and the rest of his associates had joined Beaver who was still looking dumfounded at the scattered remnants of the cord bindings.

"Holy shit," Beaver said. "They must still be here somewhere, as the main doors were locked tight, and it would have been impossible to get out."

"Well, don't just stand there! Get looking for them! And shoot on sight if need be. We can't afford any loose ends. There's far too much at stake here, not to mention our necks!"

While Johnston and his men disappeared into the inner chambers, George tapped on Sherry's shoulder and pointed to the doors. "Let's make a quick dash for the exit. We'll probably be in a far better position to ward them off from the other side."

Zoe understood what was going on and guarded their rear as they got up and rushed toward the gap in the blackened ebony doorway. Just as they reached the crevice, George heard a gunshot and within nanoseconds felt the bullet whizz by hitting the ebony structure.

Zoe dove on the floor and rolled over as if she was a commando to face the oncoming assassins, knowing full well that her weapon was far superior than anything they had to offer. Aiming at the man who had just let off a round from his Helwan pistol, she squeezed the trigger mechanism that initiated an intense, red-hot laser beam that shot out of the metallic barrel. As soon as it had discharged, one could hear the weapon click and buzz as it instantly recharged for the next delivery. The energy stored within this weapon must have been substantial and probably similar to what was used to power Zoe's ship.

The effectiveness of her weapon was mind-blowing, as Selim's thug never even knew what hit him. The laser incinerated all the organs of his chest cavity, as the beam easily penetrated surrounding flesh and bones and passed right through his skeletal chassis causing even the man behind him to suffer catastrophic burns to his left arm and fall to the ground writhing in agony.

Beaver had been running a few yards further behind the two initial casualties, and as he passed them, he grabbed one of the revolvers that had fallen to the ground and upped his pace in hot pursuit.

Zoe had lost a few vital seconds, and while she was already back on her feet and trailing behind George and Sherry, Beaver was catching up fast. Sherry reached the doors first and pushed herself through the narrow opening, followed by George. When Zoe was halfway through the gap, Beaver fired off a round grazing her exposed thigh and forcing her to limp on through. Having slightly incapacitated her Beaver pounced, bringing her to the ground and sending her weapon across the dirt floor.

George had no time to think if he was to get Zoe out of this perilous predicament. Shouting to Sherry, who had by now stopped a few yards ahead, he signaled to her to go back and grab Zoe's fallen gun. George then unhitched his dive knife from its sheath and turned to face Beaver who had Zoe in a tight headlock.

"Make a move and the girl dies!" Beaver shouted waiting for Johnston to show up, who was no doubt only a matter of seconds behind them.

Time was critical, and they needed to act now. Zoe, who also realized she would have to create some form of distraction, managed to free her right arm and grabbed hold of Beaver's balls squeezing with all her might. Unendurable pain reverberated through his body causing him to release Zoe and scream out in agony.

"You bitch!" he cried out, and just as he was about to try and reach for the revolver tucked in his baggy pants, George took the blade of his dive knife between his right-hand thumb and forefinger and launched it, propelling the blade through the air as hard as he could. George thought he might have a fifty-fifty chance of hitting Beaver remembering days when he was a kid and used to throw daggers at tree stumps, only this time it was for real.

Beaver had no time to duck as the razor-sharp point penetrated his torso and glided through a gap in his rib cage slicing through the pleural cavity into his lungs and even nicking the side of his heart. So sharp was the blade, and with the velocity that it had been thrown, that even the hilt became tightly embedded in Beaver's chest.

Still clutching onto his painful scrotum with one hand Beaver dropped to his knees and collapsed onto the ground. Blood bubbled out of his mouth. He coughed and wheezed as more blood began to fill up inside his collapsed left lung, and with his heart also gashed, he only had a matter of minutes left.

This was George's first experience at taking a life, and even though it was in an act of self-defense he nevertheless felt a certain degree of guilt for what he had just done and started shaking and wondering what he was possibly turning into. Not wanting to leave any trace of their skirmish behind, he thought he should also remove the knife, just in case.

Beaver's last images were of George sticking his right forefinger into one of the drilled-out holes in the hilt of his knife and yanking it from his thorax. He could still just about feel and hear the suction, as the knife eased out from the gaping gash.

Wiping both sides of the blade onto his jeans, George then tucked it back into his leg sheath and reached out for Zoe to give her a helping hand. She had watched the whole episode with a great sense of admiration and gratitude for being saved by her new friends. Putting her arm around George to relieve the pain from her flesh wound, they hobbled back together following Sherry through the narrow tunnel, and finally with a great sense of relief, they were out of the claustrophobic catacomb into the cool night air.

Zoe still had one more explosive charge remaining and took it out of Sherry's bag and set the dial. She indicated to them that they should leave it at the bottom of George's original crude excavation to block off the entrance. This would definitely prevent their pursuers from following and give them plenty of time to alert the authorities and try to come up with some form of radical explanation about the discovery.

Sherry told Zoe to go ahead and set the charge. Depressing the trigger, Zoe then jettisoned the explosive canister down into the void among the skeletons lying at the bottom and signaled for them to run.

Inside the cave below, Johnston had seen Beaver's lifeless form splayed out in a pool of blood and realized it might be too dangerous to consider pursuing Drake. He called out to Selim and instructed him to recover the two corpses and clean up all the remaining mess, as he suspected that Drake wouldn't take long to report their find to the local authorities and expose his illicit activities. Instead they would have to grab whatever they could from the tomb now and cover their tracks as best they could.

But soon they heard a deafening boom from the entranceway and felt the ground shake, as the explosion from Zoe's final charge collapsed the joining access tunnel, sending a plume of dust and debris into the cave. Any thoughts of escape were now dashed as they were now royally entombed and would suffer the consequences of their greed.

CHAPTER 24

Back in the valley, George headed for Johnston's Land Cruiser and found the key still in the ignition, as clearly he had not expected any resistance. Ushering Sherry and Zoe into the vehicle, he jumped into driver's seat, fired up the engine, and headed back down the rocky canyon toward town fearing Johnston may have more of his goons loitering in the vicinity. Passing the entrance to KV1, he forked left past the Valley of the Kings main parking lot and onto the road into town.

With the dive bag still close at hand, Sherry packed up her trusty flashlight that had been a real lifesaver along with Zoe's laser piece, which she had picked up following the skirmish with Beaver. Pulling out a spare T-shirt and also using her knife from the bag, she proceeded to cut up the fabric and make a quick bandage for the gash on Zoe's leg.

Zoe put her arm around Sherry, and in her language uttered, "Thank you, and thank you for releasing me from my craft."

George headed for their hotel, as they needed to clean themselves up, get some rest, and decide how to report the find to the authorities without exposing themselves and keep Zoe out of the picture. He parked the Land Cruiser in the Movenpick parking lot as discretely as possible.

As they had not checked out of their room, George asked Sherry to go to reception and get their key, as he still had blood on his jeans and didn't want to arouse any suspicion. Also, a beautiful Egyptian girl asking for her key late at night would probably add to the distraction.

When Sherry returned with the key, they walked to their room. Zoe was amazed at how this world had changed from what she had experienced after she had first crashed and could see clearly that the earth's technology was beginning to catch up with that of her own.

Once they reached their room, George locked the door securely behind them and closed the curtains.

By now it was already 3:00 a.m., and they had been on the go for well over thirty-six hours and been surviving almost purely on adrenalin.

George stripped down to his underwear and went to the bathroom to take a shower. Sherry followed him in, as did Zoe, who wanted to see and experience everything they did. As George and Sherry climbed into the large shower cubicle and turned on the water, Zoe had an urge to join them and slipped off her T-shirt and shorts, opened the glass door, and walked in. This was a wonderful new experience for her, and she enjoyed feeling the high-powered jets of water splashing over her smooth skin and gave George and Sherry a group hug giggling at the sight of them all naked together. She had not seen any nudity for over three thousand years and was beginning to get aroused.

After washing each other with soap and cleaning off all the blood and dirt accumulated over the past two days, Sherry turned off the steaming-hot water and handed out soft Egyptian-cotton towels. Once they had all dried off, they wrapped the towels around their bodies and retreated to the bedroom.

George took a look at Zoe's leg, which was now appearing much better, and bandaged another piece of his torn T-shirt around it to stem any future bleeding. As he brushed his hands against her thigh and tightened the final knot on the makeshift dressing, she felt her body get hotter and longed to be able to communicate in their language and get much closer to them both. Climbing up on to the large king-size bed, she snuck herself under the cool white sheets and cuddled up between George and Sherry.

They all slept like logs, and by the time George awoke the next morning it was already past 10:00 a.m. As Sherry and Zoe continued to rest, he picked up the phone and ordered some breakfast to be delivered to the room. As they would no doubt be extremely hungry, he ensured it was more than just continental this time round and included eggs, traditional Egyptian ful medames, and fresh falafel.

By the time breakfast arrived, everyone was up, and Sherry was trying to teach Zoe some more English words and even put a movie channel on the TV to give her some additional exposure. She was a very smart cookie and had a knack for absorbing linguistics, and George doubted it would be long before she would be able to converse with them more fluidly.

Biting on a piece of green falafel, Sherry asked what they should do next.

"I've been doing a lot of thinking, and this should now be a matter for the antiquities department. After breakfast I'll call the director general in Cairo; he actually took me on and knows me well. I can explain to him about Johnston and how he infiltrated the lost tomb, which we'd located, and that he's now trapped inside with some of his gangsters. I'll tell him that we need a backhoe excavator to dig out the collapsed entrance tunnel and suggest he have police on standby to arrest them. We should also have them search Johnston's room as well as any buildings owned by Selim, as they've probably stashed the items they took the night they tied us up. I'll also ask him to assign responsibility for this dig over to us so we can keep control and make sure we can catalogue all the treasures and restrict entry. We can also brick up the far end of the room where the collapsed wall is to keep that area out of bounds, at least for now."

"Great thinking, Sherry. Let's get the tomb emptied for now and hopefully bask in the glory, as this will be breaking news, and we'll no doubt have the international press descending on us," George said grinning at the prospect of turning a few heads back home in the UK. "Zoe can probably help us, and it would be good for her to begin blending in, although I think we'll need to try and get her some identity papers so she can eventually move around more freely. Maybe you have some contacts who can help with this?"

Sherry made the call to the antiquities department, and it took her almost an hour to convince them that their story was indeed factual and that they should take them seriously. At the end of the call, it was agreed that they should meet the department's representative at the Valley of the Kings that afternoon. The rep would have some laborers ready for them as well as a JCB excavator to gouge out the debris that now filled the collapsed entry tunnel. Armed security personnel would also be on standby to deal with any trouble.

Sherry then thanked him and suggested he make his way to Luxor, as this was going to blow his mind. Sherry hung up and gave the thumbs-up sign.

"Excellent news for once. I can't wait to get this over with and finish with all the cloak-and-dagger stuff," George said, giving Sherry a massive hug.

Looking at the dial on his Breitling Navitimer wristwatch, George said they had about two hours to get themselves ready and head back to the Valley of the Kings to meet the antiquities-department representative.

Sherry dug out some fresh clothes for Zoe consisting of a spare pair of jeans and loose-fitting short-sleeve shirt, which matched Sherry's own attire, so they really did look like sisters. George slipped on a clean pair of jeans and made sure he threw away the clothes he had been wearing the night before, which were now all in a pretty poor state.

"Incidentally, I think we should leave the dive bag here on the top shelf of the closet, as it's too big for the safe but still out of harm's way. We don't want anyone to see Zoe's laser gun, which I put inside the bag last night," Sherry suggested.

"I agree, and we shouldn't be needing it this time round, as we'll have our own security detail to head off any trouble if Johnston and his band of marauders try anything," George noted.

Feeling much more relaxed now that they were in control of their own destiny, the drive back to the Valley of the Kings progressed along with an air full of excitement, and as George drove past many of the monuments en route to their rendezvous point, Zoe explained to them as best she could more about her past life with the pharaoh and also delivered a little bit of a supplementary history lesson concerning many of the ancient sites she still related to.

Once they reached the meeting point by KV1, they found Mohammed Reza, the Luxor antiquities department regional manager, waiting for them with a truck full of laborers and also a new JCB JS200 wheeled excavator, which would follow them to the designated spot further up the empty valley to the west, which had never previously been considered of any interest, and even now, Mohammed remained skeptical, not having been privy to Sherry's earlier call.

George led the way for the convoy in Johnston's Land Cruiser, and upon reaching the site, he wondered what state it would be in. Fortunately, the desolate valley was very forgiving, and everywhere within the vicinity still looked similar. Pointing to what was now looking more like a mini moon crater carved within the sand and rock valley foundation, George signaled that they had now reached the right location and marked the spot where the operator should position the JCB to start gouging out the tunnel once again.

The machine was more than capable of excavating all the way down, as with the boom stick currently installed it had a maximum digging depth of about twenty feet. The bucket attached to the end of the boom stick could also carry up to 1.6 cubic yards of material, so it wouldn't take too long to complete the job.

After inspecting the area for himself, The JCB operator climbed back up and settled into the machine's characteristic black-and-yellow cab. Adjusting the shovel's position and ensuring he was on a level surface, he rotated the cab so it faced the point of excavation and switched over to the hydraulic control levers that manipulated the bucket and boom stick.

With each sweeping scoop, the bucket's solid metal teeth easily cut through the mix of sand and crushed rocks and removed about two and a half tons of material with every cycle. Piling it up to one side for future disposal, a deep trench formed rapidly and very soon reached the stratum where the granite slab covering had been positioned. They vividly detected the brick-lined sides of the tunnel, and after some additional gouging, the bucket began to pick up signs of crushed-bone material that had littered the floor of the tunnel.

George signaled the operator that they had reached the desired level and that they should continue the excavation by hand and clear away the remaining earth still clogging the tunnel.

Armed with pickaxes and shovels, several of the accompanying laborers were lowered into the trench to complete the job and filled small buckets, which they rotated in an efficient, chain-like fashion.

Once they reached the end of the rubble, and it became easier to push mounds of earth to the other side, George requested one of the armed security guards to join him in case there was going to be any resistance at the other end of the tunnel.

CHAPTER 25

Johnston knew too well that he had been snookered by George and had not expected that he would have been sealed in the tomb by explosives. He began to wonder who the other person was that was with them and whether the other damage inside the main hallway of the tomb had also been somehow connected. He was also extremely bothered by the nature of the wounds sustained to Selim's thugs, as he had never seen this type of trauma before. All these questions rattled through his brain as he mulled over the night's events while incarcerated in the very tomb he had expected would deliver his retirement package.

Selim was also nervous and knew too well that his boss, El Din, would disown him to protect his own ass and that he would probably have to go down in a fight rather than face a long jail sentence in an Egyptian prison, which in itself would be a fate worse than death. Ignoring Johnston now, he spoke to his men and told them to keep their weapons ready for what was going to be an inevitable outcome.

It was a long night for all of them, as their flashlights began to fade, and on top of that, they had no food or water with them, so if they were not going to be rescued soon, they were unlikely to survive more than a couple days.

Having completely lost track of time and positioning themselves close to the exit tunnel, they began to pick up a distinct trace of sounds from the other side, as the excavator dug out the blasted earth that had sealed them in the night before. When that eventually ceased, they soon detected voices cackling, as the laborers at the other end of the gravel rock face punched out the remaining subsoil avalanche.

As one of the laborer's pickaxes delivered its final sweeping blow, Johnston could make out its rusty pointed tip as it penetrated through to their side of the debris field. Sunlight cast down from the open pit, causing an intense beam of light to shine through the hole.

Johnston heard the man call out to Drake to come down and pondered what he should do, as they were about to clear out the remaining rubble separating them. Selim, meanwhile, mobilized his remaining two able-bodied men and instructed them to ready their weapons.

As the laborers pushed and scraped where they had first broken through, the size of the hole rapidly increased in size until it was big enough to accommodate an adult.

George called out to Johnston, "Hey, Johnston, are you back there? The game is over for you, and you should tell your men to throw down their guns and come out with their hands up."

"Who are you to tell me what to do? I was in charge of this dig, and you should be arrested for interfering with our work, not to mention the casualties you've inflicted and damage to the tomb. I intend to provide a full report to the antiquities department and have you jailed, along with your accomplices."

"Your report won't save you this time round. Sherifa has submitted her own account of the events leading up to this, right to the very top of the tree, and exposed you as a fraud and thief. Your hotel room is probably already being searched, along with the house belonging to your armed sidekick. I'm sure that whatever you've taken from this tomb will still be in your custody and will provide them with ample evidence to incarcerate you for many years, if not a lifetime," George retorted, now feeling in control of the situation.

Selim listened angrily and concluded that the outcome was looking more and more ominous and that he should act fast. Grasping the polished wooden grip of his own more conventional Smith & Wesson Model 29 he pondered his next move to eliminate Drake with the gun that he had so much admired since seeing it the old Dirty Harry movies.

This was very much a favored big-bore revolver packing six .44-magnum cartridges in its cylinder chamber. Raising his arm and taking direct aim at Drake, he gently squeezed the trigger. The sound was almost deafening within the confined space, and Selim's arm flung back with the gun's punishing recoil, painting the air with a silvery stream of pungent smoke, which oozed out of the highly polished blue-steel barrel.

As the .44 special round sped toward Drake at over fourteen hundred feet per second, he had no chance to avoid the outcome. Ahmed, the lead security guard positioned behind Drake, pushed him to the side. In less than a couple seconds, the metal slug narrowly missed Drake, thanks to the swift shove, and instead hit Ahmed on his left midriff, just below his arm, fortunately missing all his vital organs, though powerful enough to send him flying back.

The pain must have been excruciating, and with the noise of a second gunshot being fired, Drake dived down next to Ahmed, who was now writhing in agony, and reached out to unholster his standard-issue CZ 75 service pistol.

Drake, now much more aware of ensuring that he kept himself firmly under cover, prepared to return fire. Holding out his other arm, George reached out for Ahmed, who by now was crawling on all fours back to the gap in the entrance way leaving a trail of blood.

Johnston called out to Selim, "What the hell are you up to? You've screwed us up royally now!"

Selim ignored Johnston and fired off a third round, this time trying to take out Ahmed, who was desperately trying to keep himself out of the firing line.

Having recovered Ahmed safely from the conflict zone, Drake called to one of the laborers to carry him back up and also summoned the other security personnel for backup.

Sherry had heard the gunshots and was concerned for George's safety, and when she saw the laborer carrying out Ahmed covered in blood, she began to fear the worst. Only when they reached the Land Cruiser, where Sherry and Zoe were patiently waiting, did she comprehend that George was still among the living.

Taking over command of the topside unit, Sherry called over to Mohammed, who was still pacing up and down near the pit's entry point anxiously waiting for the situation brewing in the tunnel to get under control.

"Mohamed, can you call for some medical assistance? We need to get Ahmed bandaged up and hospitalized. This action by Johnston and his associates clearly shows his guilt, and we need to get them all into our custody and arrested right away so we can secure the site and also make sure there's a full-time security team here thereafter," Sherry said.

Zoe kept quiet throughout and was even more impressed at her newly found friends and relished what the future might bring her and that she could finally live out her life in a more normal existence, even if still stranded on another planet.

With four additional security guards now backing him up, Drake decided it was time to make a quick dash and stop Selim in his tracks. Instructing two of the guards to rapid fire their weapons in Selim's direction to keep him pinned down Drake, recounting his close quarters training with the Queens Regiment, sprinted through the hole and made a hard right attempting to circle his prey from behind.

Selim had been in tight situations before and instructed his men to return fire at the guards. After doing so, he noticed Drake's shadow from the corner of his eye. Swinging his arm around, he fired his prized weapon, which he often bragged was the most powerful handgun in the world, narrowly missing Drake, who dived for cover behind some rocks.

Drake had been carefully counting the rounds that Selim had fired off since the wounding of Ahmed and, recognizing Selim's weapon from its distinctive discharge boom, knew he had spent all six of his rounds and that this would be the best time to make a charge.

George got up and made a run for Selim, who pointed and fired again, only to hear the click of an empty chamber. George levelled up Ahmed's CZ 75, pointed it in the direction of Selim, and squeezed the trigger.

The single round hit Selim squarely in the center of his chest and sent him reeling to the ground. Blood began to seep out of the small entry wound creating a circular stain on his shirt, which grew larger and larger as more blood spouted forth. He knew right away that this was the end, as he felt a warm trickle percolate down his back from the bullet's even larger exit wound. As he attempted to talk with Drake he coughed and swallowed more of the red, metallic-tasting, viscous liquid that had made its way up his bronchial passageway.

"Better for me to go out this way," he whispered as he began to lose consciousness.

The other two goons, on seeing Selim fall to the ground, stopped firing and threw their guns to the ground not wanting to suffer the same fate as their leader.

Johnston stared at Drake wondering how he could have been outsmarted by a young and inexperienced codger and cursed him as he walked toward the security guards who were waiting for them with their guns still raised and ready to fire.

As he passed Drake, he made one final remark before being pushed out by the guards. "I'm not so stupid to think that this whole caper was just a treasure hunt to find a lost tomb. You know there's more to it, and even though I may be inconveniently incapacitated for now, I will not be put away forever. You forget, I also have friends here in high places, and I doubt they authorities will be able to keep me at bay for long, so it will just be a question of when, not if! So keep your eyes peeled, as we'll be watching you, and whatever you've found that we don't know about already, we'll eventually get to you."

"Is that a threat, Johnston?" Drake hollered back as he was being dragged away.

"Take it any way you want," Johnston screeched from a distance leaving George alone in the cave to reflect over the day's events and what Johnston had just told him.

EPILOGUE

Once Johnston and his two companions had been carted away by the Valley of the Kings security team to be processed at the local police station Sherry and Zoe joined George down in the outer cave area, along with Mohammed, so they could plan ahead how to manage the removal of all the remaining artefacts and possibly also prepare the tomb for potential future touristic purposes.

Taking Mohammed through to the main hallway, they then showed him the antechambers laden with priceless artefacts and finally the burial chamber still containing the untouched sarcophagi of both the pharaoh and his queen, knowing full well that the second mummy was actually a stand-in.

Mohammed was dumbstruck by what he saw and hailed it as the find of the century and even grander than what Howard Carter had unearthed back in 1922 when he discovered the tomb of Tutankhamun.

"We need to clear everything up and in particular remove all the mess created by Mr. Johnston," Mohammed said with a beaming smile. "As instructed by my superiors in Cairo, I'll hand over responsibility for managing this find to you, Sherifa, and anything you need to complete the task, you can ask from me. We'll have the bodies that were left behind removed and sent to the morgue in Luxor today, and once this is done, the site will be yours."

"Before we start working, I'll need Mr. Drake to be appointed as my partner for this role, as we mustn't forget, it was he who first discovered the find, and we most definitely need to give him the credit he deserves," Sherry said holding George's hand.

"Agreed. I'll make arrangements for all the necessary paperwork and permits. We'll also arrange for some temporary portacabins to be positioned here for you to work from and also put up security fencing around the entrance. We need to be extra diligent from now on. Nothing should be removed without being photographed and logged first, and once we do start moving objects, they'll need to be carefully packed and sent up to the national museum in Cairo for restoration and future display. Incidentally, we'll be inviting government officials, overseas dignitaries, as well as the international press to have their first glimpse of the site the day after tomorrow, so you have forty-eight hours to prepare for them, as this breaking news can't be held off for too long."

"That should work for us, especially if you send over enough additional staff and laborers to start cleaning up. We'll also need some temporary partitions to shield off the area where the roof collapsed in the main hallway," Sherry said, knowing full well that they would be camping there and spend many days and nights completing this wonderful historical task ahead of them that would also be their future legacy.

The valley soon became a buzz of activity with the arrival of all the temporary structures, and even the desert track leading up to the site was graded in preparation for the VIP visitors who were due the following day. Sherry involved Zoe in helping her photograph and document everything in the tomb as it was, much of which triggered long-lost memories of the time she had spent with the pharaoh, and she often wondered what might have happened if Siptah had not cut his life so short. She felt her stomach and remembered her baby, which was taken from her, and would later on discover what a great king he had become as the founder of the Eighteenth Dynasty.

Later that day a couple police officers arrived to take statements from both George and Sherry about what had happened within the tomb. They made sure that they kept Zoe well away from them and made no reference to her within their declarations. The officers remained baffled by the incredible burn injuries sustained by two of the criminals; however they did not want to deliberate any further on the matter and closed the file. They were both well aware of the presidential visit that was being arranged to see the site and as such thought it better not to involve themselves with any other loose ends.

The international press had by now arrived in droves and cordoned themselves behind the security fencing, lining up to film the arrival of all the personalities due to appear the next day and hoping to get a sneak peek inside the tomb. In the interim, George and Sherry conducted interviews and became overnight celebrities, and on the day of the official inauguration of the tomb, Sherry guided the president of Egypt through the entrance tunnel that had been the focal point of so much action, both in the present and the past. She then introduced him formally to the Pharaoh Horemosis and the most magnificent and complete treasures to be found since 1922. The tomb was also customarily numbered KV66.

Once all the VIP guests had departed, they closed off the site to any visitors to begin the task of removing all the relics and sending them up to Cairo, which would take several weeks. During this period, Zoe continued to master her command of the English language and was by now able to have complete conversations and really felt part of the team.

The three of them had long since checked out of the Movenpick having preferred to live on site in the portacabins close to where they had found Zoe. They made sure that the laser gun was carefully hidden among their belongings and that it would remain a closely guarded secret, along with their knowledge of the hidden chamber within KV66, which only they knew existed behind the collapsed wall.

Sherry eventually managed, through her network of contacts, to obtain Zoe an Egyptian identity card and passport so she would have more freedom of movement, and in addition to learning English, she was also now working on learning Arabic too.

After several weeks of cataloguing the several thousand artefacts contained inside the tomb, they decided it was time to reopen the two sarcophagi and have all the contents removed and sent to Cairo. Each sarcophagus contained three coffins with the outmost constructed of wood beautifully inlaid with gold paste and exquisitely painted while the innermost was made of solid gold. When they finally opened up the third coffin of Horemosis, his mummified remains had an additional golden head mask, similar to that of Tutankhamun, in his likeness, and on seeing it, Zoe felt a rush of sadness and shed another tear for the man she had once loved so dearly in her previous lifetime.

As they huddled together in the portacabin enjoying each other's company and reflecting on how wonderful life was, they decided that the bond that now existed between the three of them should not be broken and that they should forever remain a team while contemplating what they could involve themselves with next.

Zoe reached over to give them both a giant hug, and having previously dug back into the trusty old dive bag, which was still secured in their accommodation, she withdrew the golden ankh that she had previously clung on to for 3,500 years and asked George and Sherry to join her in holding it together as a symbol of their future life together.

Made in the USA
Monee, IL
31 October 2021